INTERN

A STEAMY OFFICE ROMANCE

HARLOW LAYNE

INTERN

A STEAMY OFFICE ROMANCE

HARLOW LAYNE

Intern

Copyright © 2018 by Harlow Layne. All rights reserved.

ISBN-13: 978-1-950044-00-9 (Ebook Edition)

ISBN-13: 978-1-950044-01-6 (Paperback Edition)

Manufactured in the United States of America.

Editor: Melita Bloomer

Proofreader: Paige Sayer Proofreading

Proofreader: Moonflower Manuscripts

Cover Design: Harlow Layne

INTERN

By
Harlow Layne

1

SADIE

As I look around at my hotel room for the night, I can't help but wonder what I'm doing. Never in my wildest dreams did I ever think I'd hire a male escort. Not only that, but I didn't hire him to take me to a high school reunion or a wedding. No, I hired my escort for sex. Hopefully fabulous sex, because that had been sorely lacking in my marriage.

It had been a little more than a year and a half since I'd last had sex. Why you ask? Because I found out that my husband, Gerald, was gay. In my vows I promised fidelity, so I promptly filed for divorce when I found my then husband in bed with another man. Maybe his vows didn't matter to him, but when I make a promise, I stick to it.

The day my divorce was finalized, I booked my

date for the night online. My best friend, Erin, had promised me that the company was totally professional. She had used them multiple times for work functions and family events to keep the vultures at bay on her love life.

What no one knew was that my best friend was gay and had moved from the state, away from her nosy and judgmental family, so that she could be with her long-time girlfriend. They had even had a private wedding ceremony that I attended last year. They were beautiful and in love, and I hated that they had to move so far away so they could be together.

From the moment I woke up this morning, I've been a ball of nerves. Tonight, I was going to have sex with a man I paid for. A man I had never met. What had my life come to?

Then at work, a new intern who is drop-dead gorgeous, spilled coffee all over my carefully planned outfit. He's a clumsy fool. From the moment he'd been hired, he never failed to drop something every time he was in my presence. Why he was still employed, I didn't know.

Probably because he's the office eye candy.

Now I wait with my nicely stained blouse and skirt on, my knee bounces when there's a knock on the door.

Imagine my surprise when I open the hotel door to find the clumsy intern leaning casually against the frame.

My knees go weak. How the hell am I going to explain this?

"Mrs. Frost?" he asks, eyes wide.

"Intern?" My mouth gapes open while my heart speeds up being in his proximity, and smelling his spicy scent.

Stepping out into the hall, I look both ways, sure that he's gotten the wrong the room.

"My name's Tyson. Tyson Jacobs."

"How can I help you Mr. Jacobs?" Taking in his long, lean frame, I try not to drool. He's well over six foot, standing a head over my five foot, seven inches. Tyson is one fine male specimen. A little young, but it never hurt to look. Wearing dark jeans with a black button-down shirt that did nothing to hide his muscular physique. His light brown hair is carefully combed to one side while normally it's a disheveled mess at the office. His light green eyes are rimmed with a dark gray that glow as they peruse me.

"Are you my client?" he asks as he peers around me into the room. Does he think there's someone else in there who hired him?

Noticing no one else is in the room, his eyes dart to

my left ring finger. Yep, nothing there, buddy. Never again.

"Your client?" I stammer.

"Did you hire an escort?"

"Um…"

"Mrs. Frost, aren't you married? I could have sworn I've seen a wedding ring on your finger at work."

Had he been checking me out at work?

"As of today, I'm officially divorced." I try not to say sadly.

Looking down the hall and then back at me, the intern skims my body from head to toe. "Can I come in?"

"Sure," I draw out as I take a step back letting him in. "Mr. Jacobs are you an escort?" I ask as I move across the room only to stop at the window.

"Indeed, I am." He laughs awkwardly as he sits on the big king size bed that takes up most of the room. "I need the money, Mrs. Frost."

"Please, I think we're past the point of you calling me Mrs. Frost. Call me Sadie, Mr. Jacobs."

A small smile graces his strong jaw. "Sadie." The way he says my name sounds like a prayer being uttered from his delicious lips.

"Call me Tyson. So…"

"Okay, Tyson, how old are you?"

"Twenty-five."

Holy shit. He's just a baby.

Fiddling with the sleeve of my shirt, I can't help but ogle him one more time. "I… think… Tyson, surely there are other ways for you to make money."

"But they don't pay as well, and I'm good at what I do." He smiles slyly at me and winks. "I'd ask how old you are, but I do know it's not proper to *ever* ask a woman her age."

"You are correct, but I'll tell you anyhow. It's only right. I asked your age," I shrug. "I'm thirty-nine."

Tyson's eyes widen as he takes me in with a new set of eyes. "You look great for thirty-nine. If I had guessed, I would have said twenty-six."

"Flattery will get you everywhere, Mr. Jacobs."

Was I flirting with him now?

Even though I'm sure he's blowing smoke up my ass, I can't help but smile. I'll take twenty-six any day.

"I can't wrap my head around the fact that *you* hired *me*."

"You're telling me. I've never done this before and then to find you on the other side of the door. Well…"

"A bit of a shock for me too." He finishes for me. Smiling softly, he asks. "Why did you hire an escort?"

Letting out a bitter laugh, I sit in the chair closest to the window. "Because I haven't had sex in close to two years, and I wanted to feel good again." Tears well up in my eyes, and the room becomes a blur. "I'm almost forty and divorced."

Moving to kneel down in front of me, Tyson takes my hands in his. "Don't cry, Sadie. You're much too beautiful to cry. Let's move over to the bed. I'm willing to bet that I can make you feel good."

"Isn't this going to make things awkward at the office?" I ask as I walk with him.

Smiling genuinely at me, he replies. "Only if you make it awkward."

"I'm being serious, Tyson." I huff out in annoyance.

"Personally, I've never worked with someone I've had sex with. I won't make it awkward if you won't. Deal?" He winks with a sexy smirk on his face.

Thoughts of my gay husband and how he was my only lover plague me. What if I'd driven him to be with a man?

My body's rigid as I sit beside him, "What if I'm not any good at this?"

"Relax," he brushes a strand of hair from the side of my face. "Surely you're not still a virgin. You *were* married." His hands find my shoulders and start to massage. His touch is divine, even if it is only on my shoulders. Or am I that desperate for the human touch?

"I'm not a virgin, but…"

"Let me take care of you. Make you feel good," he whispers into my ear.

His hot breath eases something inside of me, and I relax against his touch.

"Please," I say breathlessly.

Was that me? I sounded… sexy.

Pulling me onto his lap, Tyson begins to slowly unbutton my blouse. "Sorry about spilling coffee on you earlier today."

"Don't ruin the moment," I rush out, placing my hands to his hard chest.

His only response is to chuckle. Kissing up the side of my neck, he continues to undo each button. Slowly he slides my top from my shoulders and down my arms. His eyes feast on my see-through black lace bra.

"You have magnificent tits. I thought so from the day we met, but now…" he groans in the back of his throat as each hand cups my aching breasts. His mouth trails down the column of my neck and across my collarbone, igniting something deep inside of me.

Slowly he stands and places me down on the bed. Hovering over me for only a moment, an unnamed emotion crosses his face as he leans down to take my nipple into his mouth. The feel of his hot tongue along with the lace of my bra against my sensitive nipple sends my libido into overdrive.

"Tyson," I moan out his name.

"Does that feel good?" His voice is rough with want, turning me on even more.

"So good. Don't stop."

I feel him smile against my overheated skin.

Unable to stop myself, my hips rock against the large bulge in his strained pants.

"I don't plan to stop until I've wrung every last ounce of pleasure out of you." His lips trail a line of kisses down to the top of my skirt. Ever so slowly, he lowers the zip on the side of my skirt and peels it down my legs leaving me only in my heels, bra, and panties.

"You're so beautiful, Sadie."

My skin flushes from head to toe at his compliment. Here stands this beautiful man and he's complimenting me.

Diving down, Tyson puts his mouth to my slit and digs his tongue through my panties. His nose nudges against the spot I want him most. I moan. Pulling the fabric to the side, his tongue sweeps along my slit up to my bundle of nerves; I buck into him.

"Fuck, you're so sweet. I could eat you all night." He growls against my folds.

"Yes," I moan, arching my hips up for greater friction, and starting to ride his face.

Plunging first one finger and then two into my core, he sucks my clit into his talented mouth, pushing me over the edge. My fingers fist into his hair as I ride out the waves of pleasure. He doesn't stop until I lay spent on the bed with a sated smile on my face.

Feeling him move, I peek up at him only to find Tyson slowly stripping his clothes off. First, he fists the back of his shirt to pull it over his head and then peels his jeans down his strong, muscular thighs. Heaven help me, his body is gorgeous. I could orgasm just at the sight of him.

"What do you want from me, Sadie?"

I watch as his impressive cock juts out and bobs from between his muscular legs.

"I want your cock."

"You can have my cock, but what else do you want?" he asks as he kneels on the bed beside me.

"I don't know. I'm not used to this."

His brows furrow. "Used to what? Being asked what you like or want?"

As embarrassing as it is to say, for some reason I want to open up to Tyson. "When we *did* have sex, it was always the way Gerald wanted to do it and that was from behind. He didn't want to look at me."

"I can promise you that I very much want to look at you while I fuck you, but I want you to tell me how you want me to fuck you."

"Oh," my skin flushes in embarrassment. Now this is getting awkward. Would I be able to look at him again when I saw him in the halls at work?

"Nothing to be ashamed of. You're a grown woman who should get what she wants. Tell me, and I'll make sure you're satisfied."

"I want to straddle you and ride your beautiful cock."

"That's what I'm talking about," he smiles deviously. Sitting with his back against the headboard, Tyson once again pulls me onto his lap, and I feel his thick tip nudge my opening. Slowly I start to rock, only for him to grip my hips and stop me. "Give me a second to put a condom on."

How had I not thought about using a condom? For Christ sakes, Tyson's an escort. Who knew how many people he'd had sex with? What he might have?

"You're making me lose my mind, Sadie. I almost forgot the condom and that never happens."

"We can't have that," I murmur as he shifts, once again nudging my entrance.

"Ride me, Sadie. Fuck me hard." Tyson breathes

against my lips before he plunges his tongue into my waiting mouth.

Doing exactly what he wants, I lift up and let myself go, taking Tyson into me fully in one go.

"Oh, God," we both moan into each other's mouths.

My core stretches to try and take his massive length and girth. The pressure is unlike anything I've ever felt before.

"You're so fucking tight."

"You're so fucking big. What was I thinking?"

"You weren't thinking that's the point. Now ride me like you said you wanted to."

On shaky knees, I slowly slide up only to drop back down, taking him in fully, again and again. Each time he hits a spot inside that feels out of this world.

"You have a magical cock," I moan as tingles start to work their way down my spine. "I'm going to come again."

"Yes! Fuck me, Sadie. Fuck me hard." Who knew that the clumsy intern also has a dirty mouth?

His grip on my hips tighten as he pulls me down and thrusts up, hitting that sweet spot over and over again. His fingers dig deep enough that I know I'll have bruises the next day, I feel his cock pulse inside of me, and I hurdle over the edge, screaming out his name.

I fall gracelessly on top of him, trying to catch my breath.

"Fuck, Sadie, that was fantastic," he groans from underneath me.

Rolling off him, I let out a sated breath. "Yeah, it was."

We lay there quietly for a moment until I remember I have to pay Tyson and also see him at work.

Fumbling out of bed, I quickly start to get dressed. My clothes are scattered throughout the entire room, and I can feel Tyson's eyes on me the entire time.

"It was nice seeing you outside the office. Do you know what everyone calls you behind your back?"

My head immediately turns to look at him as he pulls on his dark jeans.

"What do they say?"

"That you're the Ice Queen of Mathers, Inc. If only they could all see this side of you." He frowns as he puts a shoe on. "Strike that. I don't want them seeing you like this."

"Thanks?"

I definitely don't want everyone at work seeing me naked. That would be a nightmare.

Moving over to my purse, I pull out the cash to pay him when his large hand covers mine. "Keep your money, Sadie."

"But…"

Shaking his head, he leans down and kisses me soft and sweet. As if we had kissed a million times before that night. "Let's keep this between me and you. Goodnight, Mrs. Frost. I'll see you at work on Monday," he winks and walks away.

2

TYSON

IT'S BEEN ONE WEEK, AND I CAN'T STOP THINKING BACK to my night with Sadie. Of course, I see her at work, but either she doesn't see me, or is avoiding me.

"Tyson, you need to stop looking at Mrs. Frost's office before she sees you and freezes you in your spot with one look."

I let out an irritated sigh. "Don't say that. She's not as bad as everyone makes her out to be."

"How would you know?" Derrick asks with a raised eyebrow.

"I don't know," I shrug. "I just do. Now leave me alone so I can get my work done before lunch. I don't want to have to shorten it because you couldn't leave me alone."

"Someone's crabby today. Maybe you need to get

laid or something." Derrick eyes me before turning and walking away to his cubicle.

If he only knew how badly I needed to get laid, and by who.

Getting back to task, I don't stop until everyone around me starts to file out of their cubbies and out to lunch. As I'm on my way, I spy Mrs. Frost standing by the elevators alone. We don't make eye contact as we silently wait for the elevator's arrival. The moment the doors close on us and we're alone, I pull her to me and kiss her as if I hadn't kissed her in a lifetime.

Her answering moan has me quickly pinning her against the wall with her legs wrapped around my waist. I grind my aching cock in her heat as she claws her nails down my back.

Breaking my lips from hers, I confess. "I haven't been able to stop thinking about Saturday night."

She pants heavily in my ear. "Me either."

I press her deeper into the wall and grate out. "I need you."

"Do you now?" she asks, with a wicked gleam in her eyes.

"Yes," I answer only for the elevator to ding. Fuck, we have a visitor.

Faster than lightening we pull apart and separate to opposite sides of the elevator a moment before two of the biggest gossips in the company get on the elevator.

Sadie peeks over at me with wide eyes. It takes everything within me to not laugh at her expression. We were almost caught. I only hope that doesn't encourage her to keep avoiding me at work.

When the doors open I stand back, waiting for the other passengers to get off before I pull her flush against me. "Please, don't avoid me."

Drawing away, Sadie bites her bottom lip. She feels guilty. *I knew it!* I wasn't imagining never seeing her alone or barely around the office.

She takes a step outside the elevator keeping her head down. "I can't lose my job."

"You won't lose your job. We'll be discreet," I call as the doors slowly slide close.

I'm not sure if I convince her or not, but I have to respect her wishes. Sadie is the only woman vice president in the company, and I can't be responsible for her losing her job. The next time we're alone, I'll have to ask her what the policy is for fraternization. I have a feeling from her reaction, it is highly frowned upon.

I need her to give me a chance, and I know just the person to talk to, to find out all the information I need.

3

SADIE

I NEVER NOTICED HOW LITTLE TIME I HAD TO MYSELF AT work, but now the intern is on my mind twenty-four seven, and I want to get some alone time with him. I'm sure he thinks I'm avoiding him again, and in reality, I haven't seen him but once in the past two weeks. A lot of that has to do with the fact that I've been holed up in my office trying to decide which sales pitch has the best chance of gaining us a client Mathers has been trying to land for the past two years. Each time we pitch to them, they politely decline and go with our competitor. I need to make the right decision, or I'm afraid my job will be on the line. There are three vice presidents of sales, and I'm the only female with a slew of men vying for my job; they would love to make it an all-boys club.

"Mrs. Frost, I'm sorry to bother you, but there's a package for you," Amanda calls through the intercom.

"Very well, Amanda. Bring it in," I snap. Did she really need to bother me only to tell me there was a package for me? Earlier I'd told her not to interrupt me unless it was important. Surely she didn't think a package warranted an intrusion of my time.

From behind my laptop, I watch as Amanda tiptoes her way into the room with a decent size box in her hands, looking sheepish. It seems she now remembers how I'm not to be bothered.

The past two weeks, I've been... I guess *harsher* is the word. One night of amazing sex, and now I'm sexually frustrated. I need Tyson's huge cock inside of me and have thought more than once to call the agency and hire him again.

"I-I was told the delivery was important, otherwise I wouldn't have bothered you, Mrs. Frost. Is there anything I can get for you while I'm here?"

"More hours in the day?"

"You've been working too many long hours these past few weeks," she smiles at me fondly.

Amanda is a great assistant, and I want to kick myself for snapping at her and being a general bitch to her the past couple of weeks.

Pulling out my purse, I grab a twenty out and hand

it to her. "Why don't you run down to Starbucks and get us both a drink and one of their delicious cake pops or something like that?"

Her mouth forms an 'O'. "You don't have to do that. I can buy my own."

"I know you can, but I want to. I'm sorry for snapping. I'm so stressed out about getting this account; it's taking up every hour that I'm awake, and I took it out on you."

"I understand, and don't worry about it. Maybe whatever's in that box will help you out. Any idea what's inside?" she asks, eying the box.

"No idea," I shake my head as I try to remember if I'm supposed to receive any packages, but I'm positive I hadn't ordered anything in the past month or two.

Waiting until Amanda is out of my office and the door is firmly shut, I grab for my scissors excitedly like a kid in a candy store. I love opening unexpected things. I open the box to find it filled with red tissue paper and the amazing scent of chocolate.

Digging in, I find a baker's box filled with brownies. My favorite. Underneath the box is a card with my name written in messy script.

I don't want to get my hopes up, but I want my package to be from Tyson. I need him to think about me as much as I have him since our rendezvous in the elevator. Slipping my finger underneath the flap, I pull out a thick cream sheet of stationary that is folded over.

Sadie,

It's been almost two weeks since I last saw you, and I hate to believe that you're avoiding me again. I know you've been working on a big project, so I'll chalk up your absence in the halls due to that. For now. As for me, I can't stop thinking about you every second of the day. The way you felt when I was deep inside you. I need you, again. I've booked our room for this Saturday night. Same time, same place. I hope to see you there.

TYSON

HOW DID TYSON KNOW THAT BROWNIES ARE MY favorite? Is it a coincidence? The real question is whether or not I'll show up on Saturday. Who am I kidding? Of course, I'll to show up. In fact, I would be finding time during the week to shop for some new lingerie.

As I go back to work nibbling on a brownie, I try not to dwell on the fact that his job is to sleep with women, and that there's a fourteen-year age difference.

I could do this.

We're only having fun.

4

TYSON

LOUNGING BACK AGAINST THE HEADBOARD WITH MY ankles crossed, I look out the window to the city lights twinkling in the dark.

I'm early.

Sadie isn't late.

I have to believe she'll be here.

It was the longest week of my life and that's saying something, all things considered. Saturday couldn't come fast enough, and now that it's finally here, I'm still waiting.

It's been almost a month since that fateful night when Sadie opened the door as my client, looking nervous. I've been attracted to her from the moment I saw her, even when I noticed her wedding ring. Obviously, I hadn't acted on my attraction until she hired me.

Her husband is an idiot for letting her go, but I won't make the same mistake he did.

Sadie is the most beautiful woman I've ever laid eyes on. Her hair is long and brown, a shade or two darker than my own with a slight wave to it, but it's her whiskey colored eyes that first caught my attention.

Every time I close my eyes, I see those whiskey eyes sparkling down at me as she rode me. Making me have an erection on a near permanent basis.

The only thing that had caused my dick to go flaccid was when I got the call that I'd been hired for another job. In all honesty most of the women who hired me didn't want sex. They wanted a man to listen to their problems, to escort them to work functions, or to make an ex-boyfriend or husband jealous. The job I was hired for was not for a nice and innocent date. No, Caroline wanted it nasty. She was my least favorite client, but she paid double for what she wanted. Before now I'd never turned her down.

I knew then that I had to quit.

After the agency's phone call about my upcoming job, I took a hard look at my finances. In a little over a month, I would find out if Mathers would take me for the position I was interning for. Unless I royally fucked up, I'd get the job. It wasn't glamorous, but it was a start with a great chance of advancing within the first six months, plus they had amazing benefits. It would be enough for me to get by. I'm a simple man who only wants to pay off his debt. Getting sick my senior year of college, and having to take an entire semester off while I focused on getting healthy, had derailed my career plans and my life. With only six more payments, my medical bills would finally be paid off, and I could breathe easier at night.

There is no way for me to be with Sadie and continue as an escort. There's always a chance someone will hire me for my body and not my company for the night. Since Sadie had hired me for that very reason, I had a feeling it would be hard to persuade her otherwise, and I needed all the luck I could get to convince her to give *us* a shot.

Looking down at my watch, my stomach drops when I notice the time. Sadie is ten minutes late. I hang my head and close my eyes feeling like a fool.

What had I been thinking?

There's no doubt in my mind that she's attracted to me. I see the way she looks at me when she doesn't think I'm looking. Maybe she sees the way I look at her and isn't ready for more than a physical relationship. She did just get out of a marriage, so I can understand not wanting anything more. I'll be whatever she needs until I can prove to her that I'm what she wants.

Another five minutes ticks by.

She isn't coming.

Standing, I gather up the box of condoms I'd purchased for the night and my keys, ready to head out the door when I hear the locking mechanism on the door click. Without thought, I move to the door in two quick strides, surprising Sadie as she slips inside looking more than a little frazzled.

She still looks beautiful.

One hand fists in her hair as I press her against the wall, while the other cups her breasts and trails down underneath her skirt until I feel the heat of her pussy. Ripping her panties away, I plunge a finger deep into her core and watch as Sadie melts into me.

"I'm sorry I was late," she apologizes breathlessly.

"You're here now and that's all that matters," I reply before my mouth meets hers and my tongue slides inside.

Heaven.

She fumbles to undo my jeans. Her hands frantic as she tries to pull them down while I finger fuck her against the wall.

"Tyson, please," she pants against my neck. The

feel of her hot breath on my skin makes me harder. "I want to feel your cock inside me."

Thrusting a second finger into her drenched pussy, I work her faster and harder. "You've got me all night. There's no rush. First, I want you to come on my fingers and show me how much you've missed me."

"I have," she moans as her pussy clenches around my fingers showing me how much. "I've missed this so much."

Crashing my lips to hers, I plunge my tongue in; sweeping through, dancing alongside hers. She thrusts against my hand as she rakes her nails down my back; I growl. I like this side of Sadie. I kiss and suck down her exquisite neck, stretching her sweet pussy in preparation.

In no time, Sadie clenches around me, her entire body trembling in my arms. Slowing my pace, I continue to draw out her pleasure as I walk us to the bed where I lay her down and promptly crawl on top of her, rubbing the seam of my pants against her core.

When she finally opens her eyes, Sadie smiles up at me with a blissful look on her beautiful face. "Why are you still dressed?" she asks happily.

Instead of answering, I stand and strip myself of my jeans and t-shirt. Joining her back on the bed, I kneel, sliding a condom on, and lift her up until her ass rests on my thighs.

Bringing her chest to mine, I hold her to me with one arm. My other hand fists in her hair forcing her neck to arch as I kiss and nip my way up to meet her lips.

"Next time I'll be gentle. I promise," I rasp out before slamming her down on my shaft. For every thrust up, Sadie slams down on me. We work perfectly together and in no time, I start to feel her flutter around me making me pound harder into her sweet pussy.

I buck one last time as her core pulses around me in waves. Groaning into her neck, I shift Sadie off me and lay her down. I stretch out beside her, still breathing heavy, and fling one arm around the curve of her waist.

"God, you're extraordinary when you come."

Blinking her eyes open, they glow in the dimly lit room. "If my brain was functional right now, I'd write a poem about how breathtaking you are while you fuck me."

"A poem, really?" An eyebrow arches as I trail the tip of my finger down her arm to the palm of her hand.

Sadie surprises me when she laces our fingers together and brings our hands to her mouth placing a gentle kiss to the back of my hand. I don't fight the smile from her affection. Maybe convincing her won't be as difficult as I imagined.

"You're inspiring," she replies, snuggling up to my side.

"You inspire me. What can I say?"

"I prefer actions over words," she purrs against my shoulder.

I'll give her action.

"Ready again?" Running my hand down her back, I continue until I'm only inches away from dipping into her pussy. I stop when I feel her body tense slightly.

Pulling back until we lock eyes, Sadie sighs. "Truthfully? No."

"Sadie, I'd never make you do something you didn't want to do. Say the word and I'll stop. I'll always stop."

"Oh, no," her eyes widen. "I wasn't…" She's frustrated as she sits up, looking down at me and taking my hand in hers. "I would never think that of you." Her eyes flicker away and when she looks at me again, her cheeks are stained pink. She speaks so softly I'm lucky to hear her words. "I'm a little sore."

Fuck.

Resting my hand on the back of her neck, I pull her down to meet my lips in a soft kiss. "You should have told me I was being too rough on you."

"Really, Tyson at the time it only felt good," she smiles in a way that I know she's telling the truth.

I was hoping with getting the hotel room for the night, I'd also get Sadie for the night. She must see something on my expression; her face softens. "If you want, we can go to my house and soak in my tub." She twirls her hair with her finger. "Maybe afterward we can..."

Interrupting her with a kiss to her delectably full and soft lips, I speak each word with a brush of my lips to hers. "We can do whatever you *need*. If you're too sore, you're too sore." I shrug. "We can always watch a movie or something."

Sadie looks thoughtfully at me for a moment, contemplating something she doesn't bother to share. When she answers me it's with a simple nod of her head before she slides off the bed and starts to get dressed.

Silently I watch her slip back into her clothing as she moves gracefully around the room. She's gorgeous as always with her long, brown hair trailing down her back, her long lean body tan from the summer sun. After getting caught looking at her a little too long, I dress quickly, more excited than I'd like to admit to see where Sadie lives.

If she knew how badly I've wanted her and for how

long, I'm sure she'd run for the hills. I need to keep reminding myself to maintain my cool until Sadie has enough time to get used to the idea of us.

"Is that okay with you?"

"Hmm?" I ask back.

"I'm going to order an Uber to pick us up."

"Oh," I slip my shoe on. "I drove so I can drive."

She slips her phone back into her purse. "Sure, I'm ready whenever you are."

The air around us has changed. Everything now seems awkward. Had I let her see too much too soon?

We're both silent as we take the elevator and make our way to the parking garage. I need to do something to rid of us of the tension that surrounds us.

The moment we're seated inside my SUV, I turn to her. "If you don't want to do this you can always back out." Not what I wanted to say, but it's out there. If she wants to go home alone then I'll have to let her.

"Why?" she asks, inspecting the interior.

"Something happened back there in the hotel room. What it is I'm not sure, but we're *off.*"

Letting out a deep breath, Sadie fidgets in her seat. "I'm sorry."

Fuck! She's going to end the night right here.

"Just drive and I'll try to explain on the way," she buckles her seatbelt and looks straight ahead.

5

SADIE

THE LOOK IN HIS EYES NEARLY KILLS ME. HE LOOKS like I killed his puppy. How this man, who could have any woman he wanted was interested in me, I would never know. He has everything going for him. He's beyond good looking. Every woman who sees him can't help but stop and stare to then fantasize about him until the end of their days. It's not only his looks that make everyone gravitate to him, but also how sweet and caring he is. A calming essence about him.

Tonight, I saw in his eyes that this wasn't a fling to him. He didn't only want sex and that scared me.

There are so many reasons for me *not* to get involved with Tyson Jacobs. First, I'm sure I'm ready for more, even after being alone for over a year. Second is the age difference. What would others think when or if they found out about us? Third, we work together. And fourth, what would happen to my heart when Tyson decides he's tired of me, or when a younger, prettier girl comes around that's interested and catches his eye? Let's not forget that he's also an escort. How can I be with a man when he's with other women? Simple. I can't.

With all the reasons not to start anything more with Tyson, there's a very good reason for me to see where this could go. For the first time in forever, I feel alive. I feel wanted and desirable. Something that had been missing in my marriage without me knowing it.

My only problem is opening up to this gorgeous man who has heartbreak written all over him. Do I put myself out there or keep to myself and my fears?

Sensing his uneasiness, I turn in my seat and produce a small smile. I'm unsure if I pull off its authenticity when Tyson's only response is the down turn to his full kissable lips.

"I'm sorry I made this weird. It was never my intention. After my failed marriage, I've learned that I need to follow my instincts, but with you I'm conflicted."

He nods, and I direct him the rest of the way to my house without explaining anymore of what's going on with internal struggle.

My house isn't much to look at from the outside,

but the inside is where it shines. Over the past nine months, I've remodeled a few rooms of my small house. I still have a lot to do, but I love each room that has been renovated. After moving out of the house Gerald and I had shared for the entirety of our marriage, I didn't want a big house. There was no need. I had no children and likely never would being almost forty-years-old and starting over.

Parking his SUV in my drive, Tyson sits unmoving, looking straight ahead. I know I need to explain. It's now or never. If I don't it's likely Tyson will drive away and never look back.

Unbuckling first my seatbelt and then his, I pry his right hand from the steering wheel, and hold it in mine. "Can we go inside and talk? I know I said I'd tell you while you drove, but this is harder than I thought it would be."

"If it's so difficult for you, then maybe I should go home." He pulls his hand from mine and moves to put the SUV into reverse.

"What if I don't want you to go home?" I confess with barely more than a whisper.

Even in the dim light from the street light, I see his Adam's apple bob. Is he nervous too?

"You've got to give me something, Sadie. I've been

going out of my mind over here wondering what the hell happened," he chokes out.

"I will. I promise, but first let's go inside. I want to be able to see you clearly when I talk to you."

"Fine, but I reserve the right to leave if you don't start talking."

"Fair enough, but I promise I'll tell you what's going on."

We silently climb out and up to my front door. I don't like the tension that's now between us, and I hate that I'm the one who put it there.

Stepping inside, I turn on a lamp on the side table, casting the room in a warm glow. I watch as Tyson takes in my home for the first time. The walls are painted two shades of grey, alternating on the walls of the room. The fireplace mantel along with my bookshelves are white and cover one wall. My couch is dark grey with big pillows that make it comfortable and relaxing. Two chairs flank the couch in a dark, purple velvet. It's one of my favorite spots in the house to sit, read, and relax.

I sit on the couch and continue to watch. With Tyson in my living room it now seems small with his large body occupying the space, but I like the way he looks here.

"I was scared I wasn't ready for more. Whatever

this is, but now…"

"You're not now?" he interrupts.

Shaking my head, I answer him. "No, when we were driving, I realized I didn't want you to walk away tonight."

Tyson sighs and sits down on the other side of the couch facing me. "What happened tonight, Sadie? If you would," he sighs again, scrubbing a hand down his face. "Just talk to me, okay? I want to understand."

"First, I want to start by saying I'm sorry for being late tonight. My mother called asking for money. Saying it was an emergency. But it's always an emergency with her. Luckily, she doesn't know my new address. She's already hit up Gerald's place hoping to find me there. As if I'd be there when he's got some boy toy flouncing around in all his naked glory." I shake my head, remembering the time I went back to get a box I'd forgotten out of the office and caught what's his name on his knees in front of my then soon to-be ex-husband. "Don't need that visual in my head again, anytime soon, or ever."

Tyson smiles and relaxes into the cushions. "So, your ex is gay?"

"Yeah," I rest my head on the back of the couch and roll it toward him. "I feel stupid for not realizing it until I caught him in the act." I try to smile, but know I fail. "I should have realized when any sex we *did* have was from behind with him not being able to look at me."

"Ouch," he grimaces. "I've got to say sex from behind can be spectacular, but…" he pauses as his eyes regard me. "I promise to always look you in the eyes."

At least he made it seem like there would be a next time.

"I sense there's more to tonight. Something's holding you back. Am I right?"

"So many things," I admit without looking at him.

When I do get the courage, Tyson's eyes regard me sadly.

"You make me feel beautiful, desirable, and wanted in ways that I've never felt before. Most importantly, you make me feel alive. I'm happy for the first time in… forever. Truly happy and all that has to mean something. Right?"

He clears his throat, but still doesn't look happy. "I'd like to think so. What's holding you back?" he swallows. "What's wrong with me?"

"Oh, Tyson," I scramble onto his lap and cup his cheeks in my hands as I look down at him. "There's nothing wrong with you. How can you think that?"

His light green eyes shutter. "You don't want me."

"I want you," I lightly kiss his full pouty lips.

"That's not the problem."

"What is?" he implores me.

"The fact that everyone wants you and once you get tired of me, you'll find someone much younger and prettier."

"Age is only a number. Don't give it power over you. Over *us*."

"I know, but," I let out a deep sigh. "This is all new to me. I'm not used to being a cougar. If it was the other way around, I probably wouldn't care."

"A cougar? Is that what you think you are?" he asks on a laugh.

"I'm the definition of a cougar, Tyson," I cry out. "There's a fourteen-year age difference."

His hand rubs up and down my back in a soothing motion. "I know, but like I said don't give the number power. From the moment I saw you in the halls at work, I've been attracted to you. I don't care how old either of us are."

"It's easy for you to say because no one's going to think badly about you for being with me," I huff.

His brows furrow. "Who's going to think because you're fucking me you're a bad person?"

"Is that all this is? Fucking?"

"I don't know, Sadie. You tell me. I want more," his jaw ticks. "But you're the one holding back."

"I have reasons," I sigh, resting my head on his shoulder.

"You have reasons, but what do you feel right now, right here, wrapped in my arms?"

"Safe, treasured, beautiful." And so much more I don't want to admit.

"All good things, so why are you holding back?"

Tears sting the back of my eyes, and I choke out my confession. "I don't want you to break me. I already feel too much."

"Hey," he says, pulling back to look at me. "I don't want to break you either. That's not the plan." Looking up at the ceiling, he mutters. "If you only knew."

"Then tell me. Maybe it will help."

"Or it will hurt my chances, and you'll run far, far away," he says, continuing to speak to the ceiling.

What could he possibly say that he thinks will make me run away?

Does he want a dozen babies?

Is he wanted by the law?

"Well, I'd like you to share, but I understand. It was hard for me to open up, and I won't push you. I haven't even told you everything."

Tyson perks up. He sits up, his hands gripping my hips. "What else is there?"

"We work in the same building, and if you continue

on, you'll be working under me on some projects. Well, I'll oversee your boss, but I'll get the final say in who's campaign we use and if I choose you, then it could be seen as favoritism."

He blows out a breath. "I hadn't thought about that."

"I have and there are options, but if we're only fucking, then there's no need for me to put into motion something that could possibly discredit me."

"I don't want that, and stop saying that we're only fucking, okay?" he growls, setting me down on the couch to stand and pace the room. "We're doing *more* than fucking. At least, I am. That's why we're having this discussion." Tyson stops with his hands on his hips. "Is there anything else?"

"One more," I bite my bottom lip not wanting to say, knowing it's a deal breaker.

"Fuck," he says defeated and sits back down, hanging his head. "It's that bad?"

"I've only been with one other man before you, and look how that turned out. He's gay," I laugh out bitterly. "It may be the way things are done now, but I don't want to share. I'm monogamous to a fault. Even though I was separated and filed for divorce, I stayed true to my vows and stayed faithful, unlike Gerald." Taking in a deep breath, I try to gather myself before letting it out. "I don't know the reasons why you're an escort, but that's a hard limit for me."

"A hard limit, huh?" he smiles, and I want to melt, but then remember all the women he has probably fucked since our first night together.

"It's non-negotiable," I state, knowing I've just ended things.

"I guess it's a good thing I quit." He smirks back at me.

Did I hear that correctly?

"What?" I know my mouth is hanging open, but really, what?

Tyson chuckles while pulling me back onto his lap. His eyes light up along with his smile.

"Let me preface this by saying nine out of ten dates were non-physical, but I knew that I couldn't be with another woman after our night together. I was notified of a date that I was less than excited about and knew what I had to do. Quit."

"Really?" I can't help but question him again because I never thought he'd quit let alone because of me.

"Really." He plants a slow and delicious kiss to my lips. "Now, why don't you show me to your bathroom where we can take that bath we were planning."

Sliding off his lap, I stand. "Follow me."

6

TYSON

SLIDING IN BEHIND SADIE, I WRAP MY ARMS AROUND her as she leans back against my chest right where she's supposed to be. Her bathtub is big enough to fit at least two more people in it and that's saying something with my six-foot two frame.

Her bathroom reminds me of the Mediterranean with different blue and green colored tiles that make up the shower and surround the tub. The rest is done in a rich, dark wood with white gleaming granite counter-tops. Normally, I would feel uncomfortable being surrounded in luxury, but Sadie makes me feel welcome. Even downstairs when there was tension between us, I felt strangely at home.

Growing up in the poor part of town has left me unaccustomed to the lifestyle that Sadie lives in. After tonight, I'd be embarrassed to have her see my shabby studio apartment.

"This is nice," she moans out. Her fingers tracing shapes on the tops of my legs.

"Are you feeling better?"

She turns to look over her shoulder. "I am. You're going to have to let me get accustomed to you."

If I had known it was a possibility to fuck her out of commission, I would have tried to be gentler.

Leaning forward, I place a kiss to the juncture between her neck and shoulder. "I'm sorry, Sadie."

"You have nothing to be sorry about. It wasn't until we were lying there and I moved that I felt how sore I was."

"I'm still sorry. Every minute, day and night, I replay our night on a loop. I've been a walking hard on." Closing my eyes, I breathe deeply. "Then I thought you weren't going to show up tonight. I was a little over zealous when I saw you step through the doorway."

My cock stirs as she skims one hand slowly down my leg. "I like that you were happy to see me." I can hear the smile in her voice.

"Very happy," I nip her neck.

"Can I ask you something?" she asks hesitantly. Her hands still their caresses and tracing shapes.

"What do you want to know?"

"You don't have to answer if you don't want to, but why *did* you escort? You said most of the time you weren't hired for sex."

"No, most of the women who hired me only wanted me to take them to events like work functions, weddings, or the occasional date to make an ex jealous, that kind of thing. We'd meet at the event, and I'd never know where they lived or see them again."

"Most?" she questions, cautiously.

"There were the occasional women that hired me only for sex. It wasn't like that in the beginning. At first, it was only dates, and after a few months, I was approached by the agency to see if I'd be open to the possibility."

Her body goes rigid at the mention of sex with other women, but I continue on. She wants to know *why* I started, not when I started to have sex for money.

"My senior year in college, I started to feel run down, and thought it was the flu that was going around until I found a lump in one of my testicles. I went to the clinic and was diagnosed with testicular cancer."

"Cancer?" she asks shocked, over her shoulder.

My only response is to nod. It's not something I like to talk about, but she needs to know why, and I'm not going to start off our relationship by lying.

"Oh my God, Tyson." Sadie turns and straddles my legs, her eyes wide. "You're okay, now aren't you?"

"Yeah, I'm healthy now."

"What are the chances of you getting cancer again?" Her voice is soft with a slight tremor.

"I have about a fifteen percent chance of a reoccurrence," I shrug as if it's not something I think about daily. What if it comes back, and what if it's too late when I find it this time? "You should know that I can't have children of my own. I don't know where this is going, but I do know that can be a deal breaker for most women."

Sadie chuckles to herself as one hand shifts through my hair. "I gave up on the dream to have children a few years ago. The barely there sex I did have wasn't producing children. Now, I'm almost forty-years old and starting over again. There's more of a chance of things going wrong the older the mother gets, so I'm okay with that. I don't need children to feel fulfilled."

"What do you need?" I ask because most women feel the need to be a mother.

She tilts her head to the side with a small smile. "To be happy and successful in life. The love of a good man who treats me right," she shrugs. "Two out of three ain't bad, right? Isn't that what the song says?"

"Song?"

What the hell is she talking about?

"Never mind, you're too young to know what I'm talking about. What about you? What do you need in life?"

"To be healthy, happy, and debt free."

"All good things. Simple."

"Simple, but not always easy to have. In six months, I'll have paid off my medical bills. Talk to me then."

"That's why you became an escort," she states with a look of astonishment in her eyes. "To pay off your bills."

"It paid the bills better than any job I found while finishing college and interning."

"What about your parents? Couldn't they help you?"

I rest my forehead to hers and shake my head. "I grew up poor. Beyond poor. My father was never around, and my mom was either working to feed us or sleeping. She never had money for insurance, and once I was in college, neither did I."

"I'm so sorry, Tyson. I hate the thought of you sick and scared, and all alone. I know about growing up poor. My mother drank every bit of money we ever had or gambled it away. I studied my ass off in high school to get the best scholarship possible to get away from her, but she always finds me, and comes begging for money. Even when I was a poor college kid, living off my scholarship money."

"Looking around your house, you'd never know."

"Thanks," she brushes her lips to mine. "I've been remodeling it since I found and bought it. Once the inside is done, I want to work on the outside. Maybe put in a pool and a small flower garden. It would be much easier with a big strapping man around to help me."

"Really?" I quirk an eyebrow.

Is she asking me to stick around and help, or is that only wishful thinking?

"Yeah," she murmurs as she starts to trail kisses across my jaw.

"Hmm," I moan when she nips just below my earlobe. Fuck, I want her so bad. My cock is rock hard between our slick, wet bodies. "I like where this is going, but if you're sore, we don't have to do this. I like talking to you almost as much as I like fucking you."

"Good," she licks down the column of my neck. "I like talking to you too, but right now, I want to ride that big cock of yours. Tell me you want me too."

"I want you so fucking bad, Sadie." A groan escapes when her hand squeezes my cock. "I... I need to grab a condom." I manage to get out as she pumps me while kissing back up the side of my neck to nibble on my bottom lip.

What is it about her that makes me turn into a pubescent teenage boy?

Luckily my jeans are close, and all Sadie has to do is lean over with her delectable ass in my face as she fishes my wallet out of the back pocket. Leaning forward, she jumps and squeals as I bite her ass.

"Give a lady some warning next time, would you?" she pants, straddling me while she works open the condom.

"Your ass is too perfect to ignore," I squeeze with both hands and rock her against my aching erection.

"I could say the same thing about yours. More than once I've wanted to bite it." Her tiny hands roll on the condom and I can't help but moan again. Her every touch drives me wild.

"What's stopped you?" I ask, gripping her hips as she positions herself above me. Sex in a bathtub is tricky business, but I'm down for it.

"Before, we were at work, and I didn't want to get called down to HR for sexual harassment."

Slowly taking every inch, Sadie throws her head back when I'm fully sheathed inside her.

"Oh," she moans and starts rocking. "You're so big. Stretching me." Slamming down, she starts to ride me leisurely. "You feel so good," she moans out each word; my cock somehow hardens while buried deep inside her.

I thrust up each time she comes down, pulling her down by her hips and grinding into her clit. Her eyes roll back into her head.

"I'm close, so close."

My thumb starts to circle her clit while she rocks against her impending orgasm. When her walls start to flutter, I pinch her bundle of nerves.

My little minx falls forward and bites my shoulder as her pussy grips me like a vice.

"Milk my cock. Just like that." My fingers dig into the flesh of her ass. "Fuck, Sadie."

My cock pulses and swells releasing wave after wave of pure unadulterated pleasure. I wrap my arms around Sadie and hold her to me as little puffs of air from her panting hit my neck, her heart beating rapidly against my chest.

When I feel her shiver from the cooling water, I shift her in my arms and stand. Her head immediately pops up with sleepy eyes looking back at me.

"Tired?" I ask as I step out of the tub and grab a towel to dry us off.

Resting her head back down on my shoulder she replies. "A good orgasm will do that to you."

"Do you want me to put you into your bed?" I ask, toweling us off as best as I can with her wrapped around me. Not that I mind, but she's sleepy, and her body pressed to mine is starting to wake my cock back up.

"I can walk," she yawns.

"And I can carry you," I state, walking her to her king-size bed with a big, fluffy white comforter on it and about a dozen colorful pillows stacked at the top.

Placing her down gently, I start to step back when Sadie's hand catches my own. "Where are you going?" she asks, peeking up at me with one eye.

I sit beside her on the bed, one arm resting behind her, and smile down at her. "To get dressed and go home."

"It's late. You can stay if you want," she mumbles as she snuggles down into her blankets.

Do I want to stay?

Hell yes, I do, but if I sleep in her bed with her, I'm not sure if I'll ever be able to sleep without her next to me. Sadie doesn't know yet how I've been obsessed with her from the moment I saw her at Mathers.

"It's fine if you don't want to stay." Shit, I must have taken too long to respond.

Kissing her on the forehead, I head downstairs. I

don't have the code to her alarm and making sure all the doors are locked is the best I can do for tonight.

When I come back into her bedroom, Sadie has a slight frown to her pink full lips. I turn off the light in the bathroom and bedroom before slipping into bed behind her and wrap my arms around her.

"You stayed," she sounds relieved.

"I only went to make sure all the doors were locked. You can go back to sleep now," I kiss her exposed shoulder. "Good night, Sadie."

Sadie doesn't utter another word but does shift back against me and wiggle her butt against my dick until it's nice and snug. I'm not sure how I'm going to be able to sleep with her ass pressed against me the whole night, but somehow, I manage to fall asleep within only a few minutes, wearing a smile on my face.

7

SADIE

"WHAT IN THE FUCK IS THAT NOISE?" TYSON ASKS from behind me. His morning wood stuffed between my legs.

"It's my alarm, silly. I have to get up and get ready for work." I lace my fingers through his hand that's resting on top of mine and bring them up for a kiss.

He groans grumpily. Tyson isn't a morning person it seems.

"Can we call in sick and stay in bed all day? I'll make it worth your while." He asks, burying his face into my hair.

"We stayed in bed all day yesterday. Don't you need some down time?" I know I sure could use the rest.

I turn in his arms to see his light green eyes sparkle down at me with mischief.

"Does it feel like I need the rest?" he asks, poking me in the stomach.

It must be nice to be twenty-five.

I shake my head and then kiss his chest in apology. "I'm sorry, but I have to go in, I've got an important meeting this afternoon."

"Fine," he pouts, resting his head on mine. "Do I have to pretend I don't know you at the office still?"

"We know each other, but you can't let on that you're my lover. At least until your hired on as a full-time employee. I don't want anyone thinking you got the job because you're sleeping with me."

Rolling me onto my back, Tyson hovers over me. His erection poking me in the thigh. "What about outside of the office?"

"You can know me as much as you'd like outside of work." I watch as his eyes blaze with something unnamed.

"Are you mine?" he asks with possession clear in his voice. "Are we exclusive?"

I rest my hands on his sculpted chest wanting to shove him away. I don't know why I'm irritated by his questions, but I am. "I'm not having sex with anyone else, and I sure as hell hope you're not either."

"We are exclusive," he demands. "I'm not having sex with anyone else, and I don't want to."

"Good," I snap and push him off me. "Now, I need to get ready for work."

"Sadie," he calls, his voice soft with uncertainty. He watches me from the bed in confusion as I step into the bathroom.

I rush through my shower not wanting to start the week off by being late and wondering what Tyson's doing since I left him puzzled in bed. The reminder of him having sex with multiple women makes me insanely jealous. I know I'm being irrational, but I can't help it.

As I start to turn off the water, I notice Tyson standing at the entrance to the shower. The only place he could see me with the all tile walls with only a curved opening for entry. His arms are stretched out above him with his legs wide apart, and one hundred percent naked.

I look at him, and melt. Tyson Jacobs is the most gorgeous man on the planet to gaze at, but on the inside, I'm learning he's just as beautiful. What's he doing with me? Every time I look at him, I want to lick every inch of him, as does every woman in the city.

"You want to tell me what happened back there? One minute I think you're going to blow me and the next…" he shakes his head wearing a frown. "You got pissed off."

Walking over to grab the towel from the warming rack, I start to dry myself while keeping my eyes trained on him. "I got jealous."

His straight brows furrow. "I'm confused. I asked you to be exclusive and you get jealous?"

"Something like that." I flash a hesitant smile. "And you didn't ask."

Removing the distance between us, Tyson pulls the towel from between my fingers and starts to dry me meticulously. Keeping his eyes on his task while staying silent. Once I'm thoroughly dry, he pulls me by the hand and leads me to sit on the bed.

Sad eyes look down at me. "Tell me what's going on. If you don't want to be with me, you only have to tell me. I thought," he croaks, his Adam's apple bobbing. "I thought we cleared this all up two nights ago."

"We did," I nod, my throat dry. "And I do want to be with you."

"Don't take this the wrong way," he sighs deeply and shakes his head. "I thought with you being almost forty, you'd be better at this."

I laugh at the bewildered look on his face. "You'd think, right? It seems I suck at this. Maybe so much that I turn men gay."

A laugh breaks through his already smiling lips. "There's no chance in that."

"I hope not because I like you," I confess.

"Good. I want you to know there's no reason for you to be jealous." His gaze slowly takes me in. "I can promise you I'm not a cheater. I like you. *A lot.* If I confessed how much, you'd run away, quit your job, and change your number."

"I doubt it," I scoffed.

A bark of laughter leaves his perfect mouth. "Woman, do you not remember just a few minutes ago?"

"If we're going to be together," I say hesitantly, biting the inside of my cheek. "You should probably know that I get a little irrational when it's close to that time of the month."

His eyes widen. "This is PMS?"

"It normally only lasts for a couple of days," I inform him with a smile. "It's worse when I'm stressed."

He nods, eyes still wide. "Good to know."

"Do you have any crazy secrets or behaviors you need to tell me about?" I ask with a curl of my lips.

"Only how much I like you, but let's wait for that."

"Well," I laugh. "You're kind of hinting at it, but I'll try to forget about it."

Leaning over, Tyson places a soft kiss to my waiting lips. "I hate to say it, but we have to get ready for work." He closes his eyes in pain. "I don't know how I'm not going to touch you at work. To pretend we're just…"

"We'll figure it out." I respond quietly, resting my forehead to his.

8

TYSON

I WATCH HER ASS SWAY AS SHE WALKS DOWN THE HALL back to her office. I swear she added a little extra sway in her step when she noticed me watching her. Adjusting myself, I step back into my cubicle to get back to work. This is going to be harder than I thought trying to stay away from Sadie while at work and not give away how much I lust after her every minute of the day.

For the past half-hour, I stare at my computer thinking about this morning with Sadie. To say I was confused would be an understatement. In all truth, I'm still confused. At one point, I thought she was going to call the whole thing off and kick me out of her house.

Standing there watching her shower had me hard

as a rock. There was nothing I wanted more than to push her up against the wall and slam into her; claiming her. But I knew that would've pushed her away, and I'm trying everything in my power to play my cards right until she can't live without me in her life.

I'm surprised when an e-mail pops up from her. Not once in all my time interning here have I received any kind of correspondence from her.

To: Tyson Jacobs <tjacobs@mathers.com>
From: Sadie Frost <sfrost@mathers.com>
Subject: 1:30 Johnson Meeting

Dear Mr. Jacobs,
After reviewing your latest proposal on the Johnson account, I have chosen you along with two others to work on this project. I will need a more in-depth proposal by the end of the week. We will be having a meeting in my office at one thirty today to discuss your ideas.

Sadie Frost
VP of Sales
Mathers Inc.

SADIE PICKED ME FOR THE JOHNSON ACCOUNT. IF I CAN prove myself with this account, then there's no doubt that I'll be hired with the possibility of an advancement right away. This could be my big break if I can concentrate with Sadie around.

In the short amount of time I've worked at Mathers, not once have I been in her office and now, after spending most of the weekend with her, I have to act as if she isn't the most beautiful woman on the planet and that I don't want to be inside of her every second of the day.

Before our meeting, I start working on my proposal. I have ideas for the project that I'm excited to share, and I make great headway by the time our meeting rolls around.

Walking in, I see that I'm the last to arrive and everyone is sitting in a small area to the right with four black leather chairs and a small table in the middle. The only seat available is directly in front of Sadie. Of course, we couldn't be at a conference table where her sinfully hot body would be hidden from me. Instead I have full view of her long legs that are crossed with an iPad in her lap as she sips from a glass of water.

I sit and give a tentative smile to the two others brought in on the account with me. From what I know, both Amy and Brent have been with the company for two years and, from the side-eye glare they send me, they aren't happy that I'm here to work with them.

"I want to start off by saying that you should be proud of yourself for being selected to work on the Johnson project. You three were picked out of twenty-three submissions. As I said in my email, I want…"

Sadie's words fade as I watch her re-cross her legs. *Is she trying to kill me?* I can't stop my eyes from roaming up and down her tan and toned legs where they end with the sexiest fucking red heels. Next time I fuck her I'm going to make her wear them the entire time I worship her body.

Sadie clears her throat pulling me out of my fantasy. "Mr. Jacobs did you hear a word I just said?"

"Yes." I fumble my pen and it lands on the floor next to Brent's feet. He rolls his eyes and then smirks to Amy. "I mean no. I'm sorry, Mrs. Frost."

Why am I always so damn clumsy when she's around? It only ever happens when she's in my proximity.

"Amy, Brent," she nods to both of them. "I want those reports on my desk first thing Friday morning. I'll have my assistant make reservations for lunch where we'll discuss how we're going to move forward." Her attention comes to me with narrowed eyes. "Mr. Jacobs if you could stay behind, I believe we have something to discuss."

"Yes, Mrs. Frost." I blush. I fucking blush like a twelve-year-old girl. I've got to get myself under control or I'm going to fuck up my chances at this job.

"What do you want to bet she chooses someone else?" Brent says none too quietly as they walk out the door.

Fuck! Is she going to take me off the project?

My gaze never leaves her as she gets up to walk over to her desk. Hitting the intercom button, Sadie levels me with a troubled look. "Amanda, hold all my calls until further notice and make sure I'm not disturbed."

"Yes, Mrs. Frost. Is there anything else I can do for you?"

"No. Just make sure I'm not interrupted."

Her eyes flick to the door before she moves around to the front of her desk and leans back against it.

"Want to tell me what happened back there, Mr. Jacobs?" Each word laced with irritation.

"You crossed your legs," I answer truthfully.

She lets out an annoyed breath and shakes her

head. "You *need* to pay attention. I don't want to be a distraction for you and have to fire you."

Fire me?

I move to stand in front of her until I'm towering over her. Now I see why they call her the Ice Queen.

"Would you really fire me?" I ask trying not to let her hear the hurt in my voice.

She closes her eyes for a brief moment, and when she looks up at me her face has softened. Back to being my Sadie. "I don't want to, but if you continue to space out for an entire meeting, then I'll have to do something. I can't show favoritism."

I nod because it's the only thing I can do in that moment.

"How about I fill you in on what you missed while you eye fucked me during the entire meeting?"

I grimace. "That bad, huh?"

"That bad." She mimics me. Her eyes move back to the door once again and when her eyes come back to mine there's a fire in them that was missing before. "How are your knees?"

"Um… good. No problems. Why?" I ask confused.

Where the hell is she going with this?

I doubt my knees have anything to do with the proposal.

"Because," she smiles as she sits on the edge of her desk. "I want you to get on your knees and lick my pussy."

Instantly I fall to my knees, my hands tracing up the length of her long legs to underneath the hem of her skirt. I slowly take my time traveling the last few inches to her sweet heat. My gaze never leaves her face as I watch her eyes burn with want for me. For my mouth.

"Are you sure this is a good idea?"

"I haven't been able to stop thinking about you all morning. I need for you to put me out of my misery."

Raising her skirt until it's up around her waist, I lick her inner thigh until I reach her soaked panties. Fuck she smells amazing. I almost cum in my pants from her smell alone and how much she wants me.

Instead, I bite the fabric and brush her clit with the ridge of my nose.

Pulling her panties aside, I slowly lick up her slit with my tongue flat until I reach her clit. I swirl my tongue, kissing her beautiful pussy as Sadie bucks and grabs onto my hair, grinding against my face.

"Fuck, yes, Tyson. Just like that," she moans with each lick and thrust of my fingers.

When I feel her clench around two of my fingers, I suck on her clit; her legs firmly clamping onto my head as she rides out her climax. Slowing my movements, I wring every last bit of pleasure out of her.

Sitting back on my heels, I adjust myself in my pants for the second time that day. There's no doubt in my mind, I'm going to be hard for the rest of today, or until I can sink into her sweet heat.

"This isn't going to help me not want you in the work place. Now, I'll always be thinking of you like this, and your face as you came all over my face."

A slow smile spreads across her face as she lazily looks down at me. "That was mind blowing. If I could, I'd keep you under my desk to do that to me every day. Unfortunately, I don't think you'll fit."

"Doubtful, but I'll happily be of service whenever you need me."

"I like the sound of that," she smiles down at me. Her eyes sated. "Thank you for that. I really needed it."

"Like I said. Happy to be of service. I should probably get back to work before they wonder what's going on in here."

"Probably. Next time we have a meeting you need to stay focused. I want you to do well on this project. I picked you because I read over your proposal, and I like your ideas the best, but you're going to have to work with Amy and Brent, and I can tell they aren't happy an intern was brought onto the project. We'll talk more about it at the meeting Friday afternoon."

"I'll try my best. I was thinking those exact thoughts until your legs crossed." I clear my throat hoping it will clear the image of her sexy as fuck legs with those heels on.

She bites her bottom lip and then blushes with a shy smile. "I'll make sure to remember that for future meetings."

Back to work.

I start to step away when she calls me back to her.

"Lean down here." Running her fingers through my hair, I close my eyes at her touch and fight desperately not to lean into her. "That's the best I can do. I didn't mean to mess up your hair."

"That's alright. I thoroughly enjoyed you messing it up. I'll walk out running my fingers through it. Everyone thinks you were in here bitching me out for spacing during the meeting, so I have a legit reason for having messy hair."

She looks thoughtful for a minute before biting her bottom lip. "Why don't you text me tonight when you get done with work? I have to leave early today for an appointment."

"I don't have your number."

"Oh, right." She looks shocked by the knowledge. "Give me your phone and I'll put my number in."

I watch as she lithely types on my phone with a mischievous grin. I want to wipe that grin off her face by shoving my cock in her mouth and watching her pretty pink lips suck me off.

An alarm goes off on her phone and for one moment I think that she's texted herself with my phone until it continues its incessant noise and a scowl forms on her face.

Standing, Sadie hands me back my phone and gathers a few files along with her purse while clearly flustered.

"Do I need to go down on you again?" I tuck my phone back in my pocket and pick up my notebook and pen.

"What?" she asks looking up at me with her cute little nose scrunched up. "No, but thank you. I... I really must go now. I'll talk to you later tonight."

She sweeps past me and to the door where she stands holding it open clearly waiting on me to leave her office. As I push past her, I speak so only she can hear. "Tonight."

From my cubicle, I watch her step onto the elevator and then lock eyes with me before the doors close, breaking the spell that she has on me.

Only it's not broken. I can still smell her on my fingers and taste her on my lips as if she was right in front of me. Under me.

Once again, I have to readjust myself and make sure no one is looking. If anyone saw how often I rearranged myself, it would be embarrassing to say the least, and I can't imagine what anyone would think was constantly getting me hard. Maybe they would think I watched porn at my desk.

Needless to say, it takes me longer than I would like to regain control of myself and get back to work. I', going to prove to everyone that I'm the right man chosen to work on the Johnson account and not let Sadie down.

Ten minutes before I'm supposed to clock out, I slip my phone out of my pocket to text Sadie only to find a message waiting for me. She must have typed it when she had my phone earlier.

TYSON,

I want you in my bed tonight.

I want to feel your body above mine.

Crushing me.

Fucking me.

Making me feel alive.

Meet me at my house tonight when you get off work. If I'm not there find the spare key under the mermaid rock in the backyard.

xoxo

I'M UP AND HEADED FOR THE ELEVATOR BEFORE I THINK to hide the bulge in my pants. Fuck! She has me acting like I'm in high school again.

But fuck if I don't love it.

9

SADIE

WHAT HAD I BEEN THINKING?

Moving the ice pack, I moan and bury my face in my pillow.

"Sadie?" Tyson calls from what sounds like downstairs.

Oh my God. I'm not ready for him to see me like this.

Stupidly, I had given him my number but didn't get his. If I had, I would have told him to go home instead of coming to my house. He would be expecting sexy times and that was not going to happen. Not tonight or in the foreseeable future.

I hear his footsteps as he makes his way upstairs and squeeze my eyes shut. This is going to be so embarrassing.

"Hey, there you are." He says from what must be

the doorway. My eyes tighten further. "Are you okay?" I hear his footstep as he moves closer.

I can't imagine what he's thinking as he takes me in. I'm in only a t-shirt with the sheet pulled up to mid-thigh with an ice pack on my lady bits.

Keeping my face buried in my pillow, I nod my head.

"Um… Are you sure?" he asks hesitantly.

I feel a light, warm touch on my ankle and assume it's his hand. It doesn't move from its spot and we both stay silent for a moment.

"Can you talk to me? At least look at me to let me know that you're okay." Now he sounds worried and I don't want him to be.

I'm worried enough for the both of us. My vagina may never work again.

Turning onto my back, I look up at him only to find Tyson's horrified eyes aimed at said area. The ice pack must have slipped when I moved. Luckily the area is now numb or at least for the time being.

"Oh my God, Sadie. What the hell happened to you?" His eyes move from my face, down there and back again in a comical fashion or at least it would be comical if it wasn't *me*.

"Surprise!" I exclaim red-faced.

Eyes wide, Tyson carefully sits next to me on the

bed and brushes a few strands of hair away from my face.

"Want to tell me what happened?" He places the ice pack back on my most sensitive parts and then covers me up with the sheet.

Why does he have to be so sweet right now?

I just want him to leave so I can suffer alone and bash myself for my stupidity.

"Do I want to? No," I shake my head. "But now that you've seen the damage, I guess I should explain."

He gives me a sweet smile that makes me want to cry. *God, he's too sweet and good for me.*

"You weren't like this, this afternoon," he rumbles with furrowed brows.

"I thought… I wanted to, I don't know." I shrug and look away. "Make things more interesting and thought you'd like it if I got waxed."

"Sweet Sadie, look at me," he coaxes.

Hesitantly I look at him to find understanding written all over his face.

"I didn't ask you to do this, and I never would," he shakes his head. "You're perfect just the way you are. We're only getting started. You don't need to worry about making things interesting." His eyes drift down to where the sheet is now covering me. "Is it supposed to look like that?"

"Oh God!" I throw my arm over my eyes. "Kill me now. No, it's not supposed to look like *that*."

"I didn't think so." He bites on his bottom lip in an attempt not to laugh.

Sitting up, I throw the sheet and ice pack off and inspect myself. "It looks better," I murmur. Some of the swelling has gone down, the redness is only about half of what it was. Thank God he didn't see it when it was as red as a boiled lobster. Unfortunately, the rash is still there and looking angrier than ever.

"It does?" he asks dubiously.

"Yeah, you should be thankful you didn't see it before. You'd probably be scarred for life. I'll understand if you never want to have sex with me again after seeing... *that*."

"You're not getting rid of me that easily. Do you want to watch a movie or something? Hungry? I could make us some dinner." He grins, looks back down, shakes his head, and then chuckles.

"What?" This was not how I expected him to act. I definitely didn't think he'd offer to make dinner.

"For pretty much the entire day I've been painfully hard. I can't tell you how many times I had to adjust myself hoping no one saw me, but now..."

"It's gone." I cover myself back up. First placing the ice pack back on and then the sheet.

"One hundred percent gone." His straight brows pull together. "That's got to be pretty fucking painful. I hate you thought you needed to do that to make things interesting for me."

I hate how insecure I am after finding my ex-husband in bed with another man and now that I somehow found myself in a relationship with the hottest and sweetest guy in the world.

"How about if we want to make things more interesting, we talk to each other before we do anything? Deal?"

"Deal." I lean over and place a chaste kiss to his scrumptious lips. "You're surprisingly good at this relationship stuff. Have you had a lot of girlfriends?"

A dazzling smile spreads across his chiseled face. "It feels natural with you, but no, I haven't had many girlfriends. Three if I count you."

Three including *me*. I'm not sure how that's possible, but I'm thankful for it.

"So, what do you say to dinner and a movie in bed? Or I can make you something and head home if that's what you want."

The hopeful look in his eyes said he doesn't want to go home. Amazingly now that sex is off the table, he still wants to take care of me. I'm so not used to having a sweet man care for me.

"I'd like that very much. I'm not sure what I've got to make dinner," I reply and am greeted to a blinding smile before he shoots off the bed and kisses the top of my head.

"Is there anything else I can get you?" he asks from the doorway. I shake my head in answer. "Okay, you relax and find us something to watch while I whip us up something."

I watch his retreating form and admire his broad shoulders and tapered waist, along with his muscular legs that are hidden underneath his work clothes.

How is it that only after spending a weekend with him I was already feeling more for him than I ever had with Gerald?

10

TYSON

I HAD TO BE DREAMING.

Soft.

Hot.

Wet.

Engulfing my shaft.

I moan not caring that this is a dream. It's heavenly and I'm surrounded by Sadie's scent. She always smells of vanilla and something else I haven't been able to put my finger on. It doesn't matter because one hint of her scent and I'm instantly hard.

I haven't had a sex dream of this magnitude in forever and decide to take advantage of it. Maybe then I won't be sporting a hard on all through work. I trail my hand down my chest and abs and encounter a head full of hair.

My eyes spring open to find Sadie between my legs with her pretty pink lips wrapped around my cock, her eyes trained on me.

She pops the tip from between her lips and smiles up at me. "Good morning. I thought instead of an alarm I'd wake you with my mouth."

Lowering her head, Sadie trails her tongue from base to tip and swirls it around the head before sucking it deep into her throat.

"Fuck," I moan. "You can wake me up like this anytime you'd like."

I fist her hair to better watch as she licks and sucks my cock like a popsicle. Up and down she bobs, swallowing me whole as she hollows her cheeks and moans around my length.

With Sadie, my stamina is that of a teenage boy and before I know it…

"I'm going to cum," I pant and grit my teeth.

Her hand cups and squeezes my balls taking me over the edge. It feels never ending as she keeps her mouth on me until I start to soften. Only then does she kiss the tip and slide up the bed to greet me with a passionate kiss.

Once we break apart, I hug her to me. "That was so hot. I wish I could reciprocate." Her reaction is to smile and snuggle deeper into my arms. It will be at least a few days before I can go down on her now that her pussy is red, raw, and swollen. "Do you have plans for tonight?"

"Just work," she mumbles sounding as if she's falling back to sleep.

Rubbing my hand down her back, I kiss the top of her head. "How about we go on a real date tonight?"

Lifting her head, she looks up at me with wide eyes. "Really? It's only Tuesday."

"Really. It doesn't matter the day. I'll take you out every day of the week if you want me to. You said we could know each other outside of the office." And I don't want her thinking that I'm only with her for the sex, no matter how great it is. "Will you have a lot of work to do tonight?"

"Probably," she sighs and starts to draw shapes below my collarbone. "I have a bunch of meetings today, so I won't have time to finish at the office."

"How about just dinner tonight and we can do something more this weekend? Where would you like to eat?" I only hope that she doesn't pick some place expensive. I need to watch what I'm spending until my medical bills are paid off and I know for sure that I'm hired for the position at Mathers.

"It's too early to think about food," she grumbles.

"But I've been wanting to try that new Mexican restaurant on Monroe street. Have you been there?"

"No, I don't make it to that area often." I shift her higher on top of me and twirl a lock of her hair with my finger.

Propping herself up on her elbow she looks down at me. "Do you want to go somewhere else?"

"No, I like Mexican." Only the area she wants to go to is upscale and pricey.

Her eyes search my face as her fingertips tentatively skate across the side of my face. "Are you okay?"

"Besides feeling you bare against me and not being able to sink into your sweet heat, I'm great." And I was because I got to spend another night sleeping in Sadie's bed, and she was currently in my arms.

"Oh, I... I'm sorry. I didn't realize." She laughs bitterly as she slides off me and sits up with the sheet around her. "I could have walked around the house naked all day with Gerald and he wouldn't have cared. Of course, now we know why. I'm not used to turning a man on with my body, so I didn't think."

Grabbing the sheet, I pull her down until her lips meet mine. "Everything you do turns me on. Naked or fully clothed, I only have to smell your scent, and I'm hard."

A soft smile spreads across her face. "I'm the same

way with you. Well," she tilts her head to the side. "I get wet instead of hard."

Closing my eyes, I moan. "Don't say things like that when I can't fuck you. I really wish you wouldn't have waxed yourself."

She laughs, and I love the sound of her sweet laugh. It brightens my day every time I hear it. "You and me both. I read that being waxed makes you more sensitive down there and makes your sex better, but fuck that. It's not worth it."

"Is it not already great?"

"Better than great. It's the best of my life. I've only been with one other man, but I'd happily..." she cuts herself off with wide eyes. Getting up from the bed, she walks into her closet, calling out. "We should get ready for work. You need time to go home and change."

I follow wanting to know what she was going to say. She's sorting through her work clothes trying to find something that I'm sure will keep me hard for the entire day. When she turns around, her pussy still looks raw as if boiling water had been poured on it without the blisters. It's that bad and I try to hide my reaction as best I can.

"Maybe you should go to the doctor," I suggest.

"If I had time today, I would," she chuckles to herself. "Funnily enough I was just there yesterday."

I look at her in question. "Why? Are you okay?"

"I'm fine. I went to see about getting on birth control. I figured with all the sex we're having I should take some precaution just in case. I made the appointment before I knew."

The thought of being inside of her without a condom does strange things to me. Never had I wanted to be bare when I was with someone, but now that the thought had been put into my head, I wanted it more than anything.

Needing to change the subject, I ask. "What were you going to say when we were in bed?"

Her cheeks pink as she pulls on a skirt. "That if sex is like that normally, I'd happily have that great of sex for the rest of my life."

"That's not normal."

Her eyes dart away as she mutters, "I guess I'll just have to keep you in my bed forever then."

Keeping a safe distance so I don't ravage her right here and now, seeing her topless, I tell Sadie. "I wouldn't be opposed to that plan."

Placing one high heel on at a time, she regards me from her spot in the closet. "You really aren't like most men I'm used to hearing about."

Crossing my arms, I notice Sadie eyeing me appreciatively. "What are most men like?"

"Closed down," she shrugs before putting on a lacy, red, see-through bra. "They don't talk about their emotions."

"And how does that work out for them?"

"I don't really have a lot of friends, so I don't have much experience with girlfriends talking and divulging all their secrets about men. My best friend is gay, but what I do know is it typically frustrates the woman and there's some misunderstanding."

"I don't want there to be any misunderstandings between us. I know what I want, and I'm going to make sure I get it."

Slipping on a dark red silk shirt, Sadie walks to stand in front of me with a smile playing across her lips. "I like that. I like you, Tyson Jacobs," she wraps her arms around my neck, looking up at me before she lets out a yawn and covers her mouth, looking a little sheepish. "Sorry, that Benadryl I took last night is still kicking my ass. Today's not going to be fun, but we really need to get moving. Feel free to shower or whatever you need to do. I'm going to go make some coffee."

As Sadie starts to slip by me, I catch her arm. "Are you not going to wear underwear to work?"

"Oh," she blushes. "Yeah, until the seventh circle of hell clears up down there, I won't be wearing underwear. It's too uncomfortable, but I'm wearing a long enough skirt that I won't be flashing anyone."

Holy fucking hell. She's trying to kill me.

"Is your goal in life to make me constantly hard?" I groan and let her by.

There's no hiding how much she wants me as she slowly takes me in. "I think it's kind of sweet."

"My sweet Sadie, there's nothing sweet about how badly my dick wants inside of you. It's manly and rugged, and…"

"You are all man, Mr. Jacobs," she pats my chest. Her hand lingers and she licks her lips. "But I still think it's sweet. For the first time in… forever, I feel wanted," she finishes softly.

Why did that asshole marry her if he knew he was gay? Does he know the damage he's done to her?

"Hey," I pull her into my arms and press my body to hers as I slide my tongue into her waiting mouth. I kiss her slowly and deeply, showing her how much I want her, and letting her know how much I care. Pulling back enough to look down at her, I cup her cheek. "It's manly and… sweet."

Sadie throws her head back and laughs, hanging onto me as if I'm her life line. I love to watch her laugh and be happy. At the office she's always so serious. Hence the reason why she's known as the Ice Queen.

When she sobers some, Sadie pulls me down at the same time getting up on her tippy toes to kiss me.

My lips part and this time our kiss feels different. I could feel her give all of herself to me.

I'm breaking through.

11

SADIE

WAITING FOR EVERYONE TO JOIN ME FOR OUR LUNCH meeting, I look up and I'm shocked when I see Tyson walk in. His movements are sluggish as he greets the hostess. His light green eyes light up when the hostess indicates where our table is and he spots me. The closer he walks toward me I notice he has bags under his eyes. Even looking as if he hasn't slept the whole week, Tyson's still drop dead gorgeous; my sex clenches at the sight of him.

I arch a brow when he takes the furthest seat from me.

He pulls out a report and pen before looking over at me and clearing his throat. "I'm trying to be on top of my game here, and with one whiff of your vanilla and whatever else scent, I'm going to be a goner."

I had no idea that I had a smell Tyson liked. It must be the lotion that I use every day.

"I don't mean to sound like a bitch, but you look like you haven't slept in days."

He tries to smile but fails. Instead he closes his eyes and leans against his hand, murmuring, "Keep talking. Maybe I can get a few minutes before the other two get here."

He really does look as if he could fall asleep any second now.

"Am I that boring?"

Tyson's eyes open in alarm. "No! God, no. You're far from boring. I've barely slept since I left Tuesday morning."

I know the feeling. Since Tyson hadn't been in my bed this past week, I couldn't get comfortable or fall asleep for long. Each morning, I used an eye mask to hide the wrinkles and dark circles under my eyes and drank an entire pot of coffee before heading out to work.

"Are you going to be able to participate in this meeting?"

From the corner of my eye, I see Brent and Amy walk in and spot us.

"Yeah, I'll be fine. Amy's perfume will keep me awake," he grumbles.

"Let's talk after the meeting. Time to get professional," I say quietly enough for only him to hear.

An hour and a half later, we've made progress on the account. I picked which ideas from each that would work and gave them their next deadline.

We're almost to the door when I turn to Tyson and place my hand on his bicep. I love the way it flexes underneath my touch. "Why don't you come over tonight and we both get some sleep?"

Brushing his lips against my ear, he answers. "That sounds great."

A shiver trails down my entire body from only one small touch.

"You want me," he states. "I can't wait until I sink deep inside of you."

Fuck.

I did want him. Always. But he was not going to like the news I had to tell him.

"Um… It's a whole different crime scene down there now."

Taking a step back, his straight brows pull together as his gaze aims straight to between my thighs. Thank God, Amy and Brent already left. "What? When I asked you about it the other day you said you were mostly healed."

"Walk me out and I'll tell you, I have to get back to the office for a conference call."

Once outside, we see that the weather has turned dark, dreary, and misty, Tyson places his hand to the small of my back and ushers me to the nearest cab. "I'll see you back at the office."

"We can share unless you drove." The restaurant isn't far from the office, but if we walk back, we'll be wet and miserable for the rest of the day.

"Are you sure?" he asks, looking around most probably for Amy and Brent.

"I'm sure. Hop in."

Sliding in next to me, Tyson doesn't leave any room between us. Instead, he puts his arm around my shoulders and draws me closer until my head rests on his shoulder.

"That's better," he mutters, burying his face in my hair. "I missed you."

A smile tips my lips. "I missed you too."

"What's this crime scene you mentioned going on in your pants? Or should I say skirt? Please tell me you have underwear on right now." He moans, sounding as if he's in pain.

"I can assure you that I do in fact have on underwear. They're pink and lacy."

Tyson groans from beside me. "No more. You're

killing me as I picture your hot body in nothing but those panties."

"Sorry." Not sorry.

"Tell me about this crime scene."

"Do you remember when I went a little crazy last week when you mentioned being exclusive?"

His body tenses at the mere mention of how irrational I was. I'm lucky it didn't scare him off.

"I remember. I didn't know what was happening at the time. Actually, I still don't, but that's crazy for you."

Pulling back, I glare at him. "Not crazy, irrational. I can't explain it. It's like something else takes over."

"So, your possessed," he chuckles softly in my ear.

"In a way," I agree. "I told you that I get that way right before my period. The bad news is the older I get the worse my period seems to get. I was hoping that once I started taking the pill it would help, but my doctor said it could cause blood clots and other problems. She advised that since I haven't been on birth control before, we continue to use condoms."

"Whatever's best for your health," he agrees. "What about…"

"Oh, that's what I call my period. It's pretty bad the first couple of days and it reminds me of a crime scene."

He makes a noise of disgust and I laugh.

"Surely you've had girlfriends and were around them when they were on their periods."

"I grew up with my mother, but she didn't broadcast it and now that I think about it my girlfriend in college turned into a bitch, picked a fight, and then stayed away."

"Well, I'm not going to hide it from you. If you want to stay away during that time that's your prerogative, but as a woman I can tell you it sucks and rules my life. I sat in my office all day yesterday with a heating pad because of my cramps."

Tyson might not like it, but I wasn't going to lie or hide what I had to deal with every month. It's up to him on whether or not he's going to be around or not.

I guess I'll find out tonight.

12

TYSON

SLINGING MY BAG OVER MY SHOULDER, I WALK UP TO Sadie's door. I wasn't sure how she'd take me bringing an overnight bag, but she did ask me to stay the night. If it was up to me, I'd never leave.

My smile drops at Sadie's wide eyes when she opens the front door. "Sadie?"

"Hey," she exclaims, opening the door wider. "I was about to order some takeout. I was thinking Chinese, but we can have something different if you want."

Following her to the kitchen, she spreads takeout menus all over the counter before looking up at me. "Whatever you want."

I start looking over the menus. I think she literally has one for every restaurant that will deliver in town. "Can I ask you something?"

"Sure. Do you want a beer, wine, or something stronger with dinner?"

Confused, I ask. "Did you not want me to come over tonight?"

Mouth falling open, Sadie's fingers touch her parted lips. "Why would you ask that? I asked you here."

I can feel my brows knit together. Yes, she did ask me, but she was also shocked to see me. Sadie's giving me whiplash.

"I know you did, but you were shocked to see me at your door tonight."

Coughing, Sadie looks back down at the menus. "I didn't think you'd show up when you knew sex was off the table."

"That doesn't mean we can't do other things like dinner and watching a movie. There are other things we can do besides have sex. I like being around you."

Obviously, I hadn't done a very good job of showing her that I wanted more from her than sex.

"I'm glad you're here. You're not the only one who hasn't been sleeping. I like you in my bed and being in your arms," she confesses with a slight blush to her cheeks.

"Can we still make out?"

Her eyes shimmer with amusement. "I think that can be arranged."

"Maybe a little boob action?"

"Tyson," she swats me on the stomach.

"What? I love your boobs. They're spectacular."

An uncertain smile tips her lips as she looks down her body. I hate that she's unused to compliments, but I'm going to keep saying them until she believes me. Until she knows just how remarkable she really is inside and out.

"I don't know about you, but I'm really hungry."

She's had enough for today, so I'll let her change the subject, and I *am* hungry.

"Whatever you want. If you want Chinese, we'll do Chinese."

"Friday is Chinese night."

I scan over the menu and pick. "I'll have the Hunan beef and the Dandan noodles."

"You like it spicy huh? Cool. Why don't you go pick us something to watch, and I'll call it in?"

Heading into the living room, I turn on the TV to find something to watch although I have no idea what she likes. To save money, I don't have cable, satellite, or internet at home. If I need internet, I hotspot or go to the library. I can't remember the last time I watched a movie or TV show besides the other night with Sadie.

Sitting beside me, Sadie curls her legs to her side and hugs a pillow to her chest. "Didn't find anything that piqued your interest?"

I can't help but smile over at her. She's so different away from the office. Tonight, she's in yoga pants that showcase her pert ass and an oversized sweatshirt that hangs off one shoulder. At the office she wears sexy as hell skirts and blouses with high heels that have all the men in the company panting.

Sadie's phone goes off and she's quick to silence it with a swift look my way.

Shaking my head, I look back at the TV and answer. "I don't really watch much so I have no idea. Whatever you want is fine."

"Normally I put it on The Food Network and wish I could come up with the recipes they do. Even the kids are better than me."

Taking the remote from me, Sadie pushes a couple of buttons and the weather is replaced with a bunch of cooks running all over the place franticly.

Again, her phone pings with a notification. Sadie looks at it with annoyance before shutting her phone off and throwing it on the table. What is she hiding?

Did she find someone else this week?

Had someone else been keeping her up all night?

Getting comfortable, Sadie snuggles up to me,

resting her head on my shoulder. Instantly her body relaxes. Melting into mine. Right where she belongs.

"How did you sleep this week?" I ask, hoping that I'm right that she couldn't sleep without me, and not that some other man was keeping her up by worshiping her body.

"Honestly?" she asks, sitting up to look at me. "Not good at all. My bed felt wrong, and I couldn't get comfortable. It was actually quite annoying."

Hearing her words, I do feel bad about her not being able to sleep. I can't help feeling relieved it wasn't because she was with someone else. But why is she acting so strange about her messages a minute ago? Wrapping my arms around her I pull her closer. "Is that the reason you asked me here tonight? So you can get some sleep?"

Shaking her head, she smiles sweetly up at me. "I like being with you, and I wanted *you* to get some sleep. You looked like a zombie today when you walked into the restaurant."

Leaning in, she kisses me tenderly. Not at all what I was expecting. I sweep my thumb over her cheek as her mouth slowly moves over mine. I'm letting her set the pace. I love the feel of her body pressed up against mine.

Her lips are pillowy soft as she brushes them back

and forth. I can't stop my moan when the tip of her tongue strokes over my bottom lip. I open, ready for her, and when our tongues start to dance together, I'm instantly hard for her. A hum starts to buzz through my body with each sweep of our tongues. I want to lay her down and ravish her, only to remember I can't. This is going to be torture but what sweet torture it is. I can't get enough of her.

My fingers tangle in her hair as I angle the kiss for better access and gently pull. My other hand softly cups her breasts through her shirt and I feel her hardened nipples. I pull her shirt up until her perky breasts are revealed. Dipping down I pull her peak into my mouth; she moans my name.

A surge of possessiveness blasts through me. She's mine, and I want to claim her. It's been too long.

Dingdong.

My head whips to the door, and I think I might have actually growled.

"Easy there tiger." Sadie soothes from underneath me. "It's our dinner, and as much as I was thoroughly enjoying your mouth, I'm hungry. Raincheck?"

Sitting up, I pull her with me. "Raincheck." I murmur, disappointed.

A few minutes later, Sadie's back with plates and silverware along with our food ready to dig in.

Eyeing the small amount on my plate, she laughs. "Oh, that's all for you. I can't do spicy so eat up."

We sit and watch a show called *Chopped* while eating our Chinese, and it amazes me what the chefs can cook in the short amount of time they're given, and with such strange ingredients. If it was me, I would've taken the entire time coming up with an idea.

In the distance, Sadie's home phone rings, I watch her as she looks over her shoulder at the sound.

"Do you need to get that?"

"No," she shakes her head. "I wish I didn't need a home phone for my security. Looks like I'm going to have to change both my numbers. Again." Her mouth's in a thin line as she stares at the cooking show.

Why would she need to change her numbers? Did she meet some dude, and he won't leave her alone now? She's had to do it more than once?

Turning toward her with drawn brows, I can't hide my apprehension. "Can I ask?"

"Of course, you can ask. I'm sure you think I'm acting like a crazy person or worse. It's my mother. She's been calling and texting nonstop all week. I don't answer because I know what she wants. Money," she twirls a lock of her hair around her finger. "It's always money. I don't know how she keeps getting my phone numbers. I have them private, and yet she still seems to miraculously get them every time."

"You could block her on your cell phone." I'm not sure what she could do about her home phone.

Her eyes light up. "I should. Why didn't I think of that? Probably because I've been so damn tired this week."

Hopefully now that I'm here we'll both get some much needed sleep.

Leaning back, Sadie moans and places her hands on her belly. "I'm so full I have a food baby."

Far from it, but it's cute she thinks so.

"Now that I'm full, I think I might pass out now that you're with me." I lean back and close my eyes.

"Sleep sounds like a good idea," she murmurs, leaning her head against my shoulder and throwing a blanket over us.

Opening one eye, I look down at her snuggled up to me with a serene smile on her face. "You want to sleep here?"

"Just a nap. I don't want to move," she grumbles.

I can't fault her. I'm warm, full, and have Sadie in my arms.

My world starts to slowly fade away as I listen to her breathing become slow and steady. She's asleep, and in only a few moments, so am I.

For the first time in days, we both sleep all night wrapped in each other's arms.

13

SADIE

TYSON KNOCKS ON MY OFFICE DOOR AND THEN POKES his head in. "You wanted to see me, Mrs. Frost?"

"Yes, please come inside and close the door behind you," I say sternly. The past month it has been hard to hide how I feel about Tyson at the office, so I decided no more Mrs. Nice Boss, not that I ever was one, but I'm especially hard on Tyson. And from what he's said, everyone noticed and wondered what he did to piss me off.

He stalks toward me with no emotion on his face. As if he hadn't woken me up this morning with his head between my thighs until I came all over his face and fingers.

My lights are off with the only light coming from the floor-to-ceiling windows that look out over the city.

I love to look out and see the busy city throughout my day, and the twinkling lights at night. Although there haven't been too many late nights at the office since Tyson came into my life.

Speaking of Tyson, he stands in front of my desk with his hands clasped in front as he stares straight ahead waiting for me to acknowledge him again or to offer him a seat.

"Mr. Jacobs, please sit. I'd like to go over a few things with you." I shuffle the papers on my desk and stack them at the corner of my desk.

His eyes widen for the briefest of moments before he takes a seat. I watch as he places his clasped hands on one knee and keeps his stoic expression.

"First, I wanted to inform you that Mathers will be installing a more sophisticated security system throughout the building. Everyone will be required to use their assigned keycard in the lobby along with several other places throughout the building." Tyson raises an eyebrow in question. I'm sure he's wondering why I'm telling him this. "Part of the upgrade will be security cameras placed strategically throughout the building."

He clears his throat and looks around the room.

"As far as I know there aren't any cameras in my office. I do know there will be some in the stairwells, and in front of the elevators, but that's as far as my knowledge goes."

This means that Tyson and I will have to keep a strictly professional relationship while at work.

"Do they know?" he shakes his head. "No, that would be a pretty extreme measure just to catch your employees in a compromising situation."

"Oh, they're looking to catch employees, but not us. There have been multiple expensive items that have gone missing from Mathers, and they're going to do everything in their power to catch who it is. The cameras will be installed this weekend while everyone is gone, and no one will be the wiser. The keycard system will take a little longer, but it will be in plain sight."

His straight brows cinch. "Is that why you called me in? It could have waited until we got home." His mouth clamps shut, and he looks everywhere but me.

In the past month, Tyson hasn't spent a night in his own bed. He's gone back to his apartment to pick up clothes and toiletries, but that's it. In all honesty, I have no idea what could possibly be left there. We're living together without officially living together. I've thought about asking him, but at the mention of home, he starts acting weird just as he is right now. I think he's afraid I'm going to tell him I want him to leave and to not come back.

I let it slide for now and I'll bring it up when he can't ignore me. When he's fucking me, he can't look away. Well, he could, but he won't. Not after I told him about how Gerald would never look at me when we had sex.

"That's not the only reason, but I wanted you to know. We're going to have to be even more careful from now on."

Tyson's jaw ticks, but he doesn't speak.

I know that he wants to come out as a couple and hates sneaking around, but we needed to keep it a secret until he was hired. Now we need to give it a little more time *if* he accepts the job, I'm about to tell him about.

"Tyson," I sigh his name. Hating that it hurts him that no one knows about us. "I know you don't like hiding, but it's not forever. I promise."

"I know," he snaps, childishly. Eyes trained to the city landscape outside my office.

Again, I don't say anything because I don't want to fight with him at work and I do understand why he's upset.

"I also called you in here to let you know that after a long meeting about the Johnson account, we have decided to go with your idea and make you team leader."

"Really?" he perks up.

"And there's more," I lead, loving the sight of him so happy and enthused.

"Do I have to bend you over your desk and fuck you for you to tell me?" he asks with a twinkle in his eye. He would love to do just that, but I don't want the entire sixteenth floor hearing us.

The smile that blooms across my face, I don't bother to hide. Instead I shake my head and lean back in my chair. "If you accept, you're no longer an intern here at Mathers, but a full-time employee, and because they like your ideas and hard work, you'll be starting out with a salary of forty-five thousand dollars and a bonus."

Tyson sits in shock, opening and closing his mouth for a few moments before he stands and spills out. "Holy fucking shit, Sadie! Did you do this?"

Standing, I make my way to the front of my desk and in front of Tyson, placing my hands on his firm chest. "It was all you. I only told them the truth about what I've witnessed from you. If you keep it up, you'll soon be stealing my job."

"This is some of the best news I've ever heard. Right after finding out I was cancer-free."

Pulling me flush against his tall, muscular frame, he circles me in his arms. I can't help but rest my head on his glorious chest. The feel of his tight muscles bunch as he pulls me closer and the sound of his heart beating are perfect. I could stay in his arms forever, if he'd let me.

"I got the job," he whispers to himself. "Now, I can…" Tyson cuts himself off, looking down at me with a smile plastered on his face. "I got the fucking job."

"You did. I'm so proud of you. You've worked your ass off day and night. We should celebrate. Go out to dinner or a night on the town this weekend or both."

"And I'm paying," he says with a scowl.

Since Tyson quit his escorting job, he's been a little short on spending cash and absolutely hates it when I buy dinner almost every night. In a way, I find it sweet. Gerald let me pay for *everything*, and I mean everything, once I started to make more money than he did. Luckily for me, he only got the house in the divorce. Not that I wanted to live in the place where he'd cheated on me. Who knows how many times he'd had sex with other people in my own bed.

"If you want to pay, then I'll let you pay. I don't do it for any other reason than I know that you barely make any money as an intern."

Skimming his thumb along my cheekbone, I lean into his touch.

"When does this go into effect?"

Taking a step back before we get lost in each other, I answer him. "Tomorrow."

"So soon?" his eyes light with excitement. "When will Brent and Amy find out I'll be their leader?"

"At Friday's meeting, so be prepared for them to hate you more."

"They really are assholes. The only people they can work with without making everyone miserable are each other."

"If they weren't good at their jobs, they'd have been fired by now. Enough talk about them though. Where do you want to go to dinner tonight?"

Tilting his head to the side, he purses his kissable lips. "Can I let you know? I wasn't expecting this."

"Yeah, I'm just hungry and ready to get out of here. The lunch they had catered for our meeting was cold and unappetizing."

"You should have had lunch with me in the cafeteria."

"Anything would have been better, even the cafeteria food. I'm going to sit at my desk and dream of food until it's time to leave."

"I'm sure I could give you something to think about instead of food," he growls with a roguish glint in his eyes.

My hands to his chest, I push him away giggling. "Down boy. You can wait until tonight."

Tyson groans, placing his large hands on my hips and pulling me into him until he can grind his cock against me. "Why can't I get enough of you?"

"Because you're male and young," I laugh, trying to push him away again and failing.

"I've never wanted anyone as much as I want you. Don't deny me, Sadie." His hands glide up from my waist and up my back until one wraps around the back of my neck and the other snakes through my hair.

"Just a kiss," he begs, eyes on fire.

Before I have a chance to answer Tyson must see my will crumble, because in the next second he's on me. Full lips move against mine, forcefully parting them. His tongue darts inside, domineering the moment.

I'm his.

I have been from the moment he slid inside of me back in that hotel room months ago.

He tastes every inch of my mouth, turning my head to get me where he needs me as I'm devoured.

It's our hottest kiss yet. I don't want it to stop. I want him to bend me over my desk and take me.

He grinds his thick cock against me, reading my mind.

"Ty," I moan as my hands roam the broad expanse of his back.

"Ms. Frost," Amanda interrupts through the intercom. "I'm sorry to disrupt your meeting, but you have an important call on line one."

"Tonight," Tyson pecks my lips once, twice, three times before pulling back. "We'll be finishing this."

"Yes, sir," I answer with a slap to his firm ass.

THE NEXT DAY, I'M SITTING BY MYSELF IN THE cafeteria of Mathers picking at my salad while trying to discreetly stare at my... what is Ty to me? Boyfriend seems so immature. All I know is that he's mine, even if every woman in the building flirts relentlessly with him. Since my best friend moved away, I normally sit by myself. Not that I mind. Much. Ty however sits with a crowd of people about him while they all laugh and talk about who knows what.

"Can I join you?" Amy asks, already sliding her tray onto the table.

Internally I roll my eyes. I hate her superior attitude. It has never made any sense to me. Yes, Amy's good at her job, but she's never going to get promoted acting that way around her co-workers and especially her bosses. She's already been transferred once because the other vice president couldn't stand to work with her. Trust me, that's saying a lot, because Smith is indifferent toward everyone.

"Go ahead," I motion to the chair she's lowering herself down in.

"So, I was thinking since I didn't get lead on the Johnson account, which I deserve by the way, that you should make me lead on the Mitchell account."

"Stacy is going to be lead, but if you'd like I can put you on her team. You had a few good ideas." I fork a bite of chicken, bringing it to my mouth when her next words stop me.

"It wasn't really a suggestion, but a demand," she smirks.

My back shoots ramrod straight. "A demand? What makes you think you can demand anything of me?"

"Oh, how about the fact that I know for certain that you're fucking one of your employees," her smirk widens into an evil grin.

That little bitch.

I shrug. There's no way in hell I'm letting her see that she's getting to me, or letting her blackmail me into making her lead when she doesn't deserve it. If it was up to me, I'd fire her sorry ass.

"I don't know what you're talking about."

Did I really just say that?

"Are you really going with that? You're not as sneaky as you think you are. You're lucky I'm the one that caught you."

I scoff and this time I do roll my eyes. She's delusional.

"If you don't make me the lead at the next meeting, I'm going to HR. Do you want to lose your job?" she smirks, thinking she's triumphant.

I don't know what to say. I don't want to give her any ammunition or say something that I could regret later. Instead of saying anything, I stare her down. Amy tries to hold my gaze. To beat me in this absurd game. She even takes a sip of soup, but falters when I only sit there and continue staring.

Who does this bitch think she is?

Clearing her throat, she stands with her tray. "If you don't make me lead at the next meeting, you'll regret it."

14

TYSON

MY FINGERS DIG INTO HER ASS AS I DRIVE INTO HER tight heat. Sweat starts to bead on my forehead with each precise thrust to her g-spot.

"Ty," she moans, clawing at my back. "Harder."

A beast awakens in me every time she groans out 'harder', and I lose control, slamming into the only pussy for me.

I grip her harder, knowing I'll likely leave marks on that perfect ass of hers. Pressing my forehead to the side of her neck, I pound her to release. I don't stop until her walls stop fluttering and milking my cock of every last bit of my essence.

Sadie turns and kisses the side of my face, and I in turn bury my head in the crook of her neck. Her fingers comb through my damp hair, and I can't help but moan. I love feeling her touch.

Anywhere.

Everywhere.

I crave it.

Even if it's only my hair.

"I should give you a raise more often if this is the response I get."

A dopey smile spreads across my face remembering how surprised I was when Sadie said I got the job along with the salary and bonus. I'm also heading up the team for the project. I can't believe it.

"I … I can't believe it."

Holy shit!

I almost told Sadie I loved her and at the worst possible time. Pinned up against the wall while we talk about work is not how I envisioned when I finally tell her I love her. I don't want it to be too soon and scare her off. Is it still too soon?

She's getting better about us, but I'm not willing to risk spooking her and have her shut down on me.

Setting her on her feet, I head into the bathroom and throw away the condom.

"You should believe it. You worked hard for it and you deserve it," she says from behind.

Turning, I find her standing at the entry to the

bathroom just as I left her. Completely naked and sated.

Perfection.

"Thank you," I say as I stalk toward her and scoop her in my arms. Sadie squeals and throws her arms around my neck giggling all the while. "I'm going to work harder than ever to prove you picked the right person for the job."

Placing her on the bed, she splays her body out in invitation. I can't take my eyes off her. Her smooth, silky skin. Pert tits that I want to bite and suck all day. Curvy hips that are perfect for grabbing onto while I plunge into her over and over again. Her perfect pink pussy that glistens all for me. Every inch of her is an aphrodisiac and meant only for me.

"You're beautiful," I confess for at least the hundredth time.

Her warm hand cups my cheek as she smiles up at me. "You're the one that's beautiful. Inside and out."

Laying down beside her, I twirl a lock of her hair as she draws patterns on my chest. They're always random and most of the time I have no idea what she's drawing. Probably because on the inside, I'm purring like a cat at her touch and barely pay attention.

"I still can't get over Amy threatening me. She's such a little bitch. If that's how she thinks she's going to move up in the company, she's got another thing coming."

"No one likes her. From what I've heard, she's not a good lead on projects or accounts. She won't listen to anyone's ideas but Brent's."

"Thanks for letting me know. No one's mentioned it to me," she rests her head on my shoulder.

"Because they're all scared of you," I chuckle.

I know I'm sleeping with her, but she's really not that bad at work. They make her out to be way worse than she is.

With brows furrowed, she snuggles against my side. "Can I ask you something?"

"Anything," I answer immediately.

"I've been meaning to ask, but something always comes up," her eyes dart down to my semi-erect cock and she giggles again. I can't help but smile every time I hear her sweet little giggle. "Before at the office, you were always… how do I say this? Um… clumsy?"

Fuck, I was a stumbling idiot at the office.

"It kind of balanced out everything else."

"What out?"

"Your perfection," she answers with a slight blush.

Cocking a brow, I ask with a grin. "You think I'm perfect?"

"Oh please," Sadie rolls her eyes at me. "You

know what you look like. Tall, dark, and handsome. At least when you were clumsy you seemed more human. What happened to you dropping and spilling stuff?"

Her hand stops tracing patterns and roaming, and rests over my heart. Lacing our fingers together, I kiss the top of her head.

"I was clumsy because of you. From the moment, I saw you I was attracted to you and wanted you. But I knew I couldn't have you when I saw a wedding ring on your finger. It came out as nerves. I tried to reign in what I was feeling for you, and it came out as me being a bumbling fool." Pulling her tighter against me, I rub my hand up and down her back. "Trust me, I heard the whispers and snickers about what a laughingstock I was."

She kisses my chest and looks up at me. "That's not cool. I'm sure Amy and Brent were the instigators. Those two," she shakes her head, looking cutely annoyed. "What are they saying now?"

"The typical water cooler talk, and how I must have really fucked up because you're always pissed off at me." I can't help but laugh. Sadie is far from pissed off at me. I make sure she's happily sated each and every morning and get rewarded with sweet smiles and googly eyes until we're at the office. Once we arrive a mask of indifference falls over her face and it only changes to scowl at me.

It will definitely be interesting when they find out Sadie and I are… dating? It feels like it's more than dating and at the same time it doesn't. We've only been out a couple of times instead most nights we opt for staying in, eating dinner in front of the TV while watching a movie, and then ravaging each other until late into the night.

"What's the water cooler talk?" she asks pulling me out of my musings.

Shaking my head, I laugh. "They don't know I've heard them, and you don't want to know."

Getting up to lean over me, Sadie smiles mischievously with her eyebrows raised. "Now I really want to know. You don't have to tell me what they say about me. I know it's nothing good, and I don't care. I'm their boss. I'm not there to make friends with any of them. Before I became vice president they were seriously slacking off, and I whipped them into shape. It hasn't gone unnoticed by the company." She shrugs the best she can while holding herself up on one elbow.

I wouldn't tell her what they said about her. Sadie is fierce when it comes to work, but hearing the awful things they say about her would break even the strongest.

"Do you really want to hear what they say about me?" I wasn't sure how she'd react and by my calculations it was about that time of the month for Sadie to become irrational. Or as I like to call it. Crazy.

"Are they saying mean things about you?" she scowls down at me, nostrils flaring.

What would she do if she heard what they said about me?

Curling up, I kiss the tip of her now scrunched up nose. "No, it's not *mean*." My fingers caress up and down her hip trying to calm her just in case she doesn't like what she hears. Taking in a deep breath, I close my eyes. "They speculate how large my member is. If I'm dating anyone. What it would be like to fuck me. If I'm as clumsy in bed as I am out of it. Why I'm an intern. Shit like that."

When she doesn't say anything, I open my eyes to find her looking down at me blank-faced.

"Hey, I don't care what they say," I say in a soothing tone.

Blinking a few times, she turns to look at something in the distance for a moment. "Do they think you're good in bed?"

I was not expecting that.

A chuckle escapes as I shake my head. "No. Their words, not mine, are 'He can't look like that *and* be great in bed.' But I don't care what they say about me. They talk shit about everyone."

"I, for one, am happy they don't know how phenomenal you are in bed. If they had any idea, I'd have to kill each and every one of them."

There she is. My crazy Sadie. And yet, I can't help but love that she's possessive over me.

"Let's not kill anyone at the office. I like you too much. I'd hate for you to go to prison."

"Me too," she laughs and lays back down and snuggles into me.

Her warmth against me, along with her rubbing my back, almost lulls me to sleep when her hand abruptly stops.

"Hey, Ty. We need to talk."

Dread fills my entire being and my heart sinks.

15

SADIE

TEARS STING THE BACK OF MY EYES WHEN I FEEL HIS body lock up and his arms tense around me. When I feel him try to get up, I sling my leg over his and wrap my arms tighter around him.

"Ty, please just listen." When he stops moving and stays stone still, I try to relieve him as best as I can. We needed to talk and figure this out. "It's nothing bad. I promise."

"What is it?' he asks, voice monotone.

"I've been trying to talk to you about this for some time now, but you always change the subject, or leave. If you want to be in a relationship with me, we have to talk. Now." I demand, but try to keep my voice soft.

"You know I want to be with you." His voice rumbles underneath my ear.

"I've got a pretty good indication, but we still need to talk. You haven't been back to your apartment in over a month."

"I know," he replies solemnly.

I hate to hear the sadness in his voice. Did he really think I was going to kick him out of my bed and home after the night we'd just had?

"I've been thinking about this for a while and wanted to talk to you about it, but you keep avoiding the conversation. I was going to confront you while having sex, but I'm too consumed to even think about talking about something serious, so I thought now's the perfect time."

"If you want me to leave you can tell me," he says miserably.

"I don't want you to leave, Ty." I let out a sigh. "This is difficult for me, okay? I like you. A lot. More than I should, but I can't help how I feel."

Before I know what's happening, I'm on my back with Tyson hovering over me. I can barely make out his face in the dark, but from what I can tell it is harsh and serious.

"What do you mean it's hard and more than you should?" he barks out an inch from my face.

Tears sting the backs of my eyes. "For so many

reasons. First of all, I'm your boss and second, you're the first guy I've dated or been with since the divorce." I try to push him off me, but he doesn't budge. I need some breathing room so what I want to say doesn't come out a total mess just like that.

"That came out wrong. I'm sorry. It's like I won the lottery with you. How did I get so lucky that you were the man in that hotel room? Really Ty, you're perfect. Almost. I can get over everything else, but the age difference. You're so young, and I feel like I'm going to hold you back. You should be out going to parties and clubs, not sitting around the house with me watching movies."

"Are you finished?" he asks harshly.

"You could do better," I confess.

There I said it.

"My dear beautiful, sweet Sadie," he shakes his head at me, his nose grazing mine. "You don't see yourself as I do. I don't want to do better. I only want you. I have since the moment I saw you, and nothing's going to change that."

"You can't say that. You could change your mind."

He cocks his head to the side. "Is that what you're afraid of? If you give yourself completely to me that I'll change my mind?"

"Maybe," I whisper in the dark.

"From day one, I've been all in. I know what I want, and what I want is you. I can promise you here and now that I won't change my mind. Trust me, I know it's scary. There's so much I've held back in the fear that I'd scare you away." He kisses my cheek, still hovering.

"I don't want to ruin your life. I don't want you to wake up one day and wonder why you're here with this old lady beside you."

"Between the two of us, you're the only one that's thinking of our age difference. I don't see your age. I only see you."

Turning to look out the window, I sigh. "I need to get over my hang ups. Rationally, I know that if I was in a relationship with anyone, they could get tired of me and leave me. I could do the same. There's always that chance. Or they could turn gay."

"Rarely does that happen. He was already gay before he got involved with you. The world wasn't as tolerant back then. It still isn't now in a lot of places. But that didn't give him the right to marry you when he knew better."

"How do you always say the right thing to make me feel better?" With my mind spiraling at the uncertainty of every aspect of our relationship, Tyson always calms me and my thoughts.

"Because we're perfect for each other." Burying his face into the crook of my neck, he places a sweet kiss and grazes up the column of my neck, holding me tighter. "Was that what you wanted to talk about?"

"It was something we needed to talk about, but no it wasn't what I wanted to say. If you really believe everything you just said to me then I think you'll be happy with what I'm about to ask you."

Rising up to rest his weight on his forearms, he looks down at me. I hate that it is so difficult to see his face in the dark. The only light is from the barely there moonlight.

Letting out a breath I didn't know I was holding, I bite the bullet and say what I'd been wanting to say for the past couple of weeks. "Since you haven't stayed a night in your apartment in over a month, I was thinking maybe you should move in."

"You want me to move in?" he asks in awe.

I guess it was a little surprising when I was afraid that at any moment he'd wake up and decide he could do better.

Cupping his cheek, I kiss first one eye and then the other, the tip of his nose, and finally his kissable lips.

"Only if you want to. You're already here all the time and there's no point in you paying rent on an apartment that you're never at. Plus, I don't think I could sleep in this bed if you weren't here with me."

"That's what I've been afraid of. The sleeping part, I mean. After spending one weekend with you in this bed, I couldn't sleep again until you asked for me to come back." He dips down and kisses the tip of my nose. "I would love nothing more than to live with you, but I'm going to pay my part. With the bonus, I can pay off the rest of my medical bills and still be comfortable."

I know I have to let him contribute, even if he does make a substantial amount less than I do, so I'm not going to fight him on it.

"We'll figure something out the next time the bills need to be paid," I pull him back down for another kiss. "We can get the rest of your things this weekend. How much more do you have on your lease?"

Kissing down the length of my body, Tyson looks up at me. "Only a couple of months, I wanted to get a better place when I could afford one."

Throwing one leg over his shoulder, he licks me so thoroughly I almost come right then and there. My fingers tangle in his hair as I grind my aching core against his talented mouth. Each time he starts at my opening with his tongue flat. Once he reaches my stiff bundle of nerves, he swirls and sucks only to start over again.

"Ty, I need more," I moan.

Plunging two fingers in and out in a steady tempo, he sucks and nibbles on my clit until stars burst from behind my eye lids, my legs clench against his head as I ride out every bit of my never-ending orgasm.

Moving to the side, Tyson reaches for a condom in the drawer.

"Wait," I say so softly I barely hear myself, but he must have because he stops and looks over at me. "I'm pretty sure you just agreed to move in with me, right?"

"Yeah," he answers hesitantly.

"So that means you trust me, and I trust you. I got tested and I'm clean, and you are too. We don't need to use a condom. I don't know why we've been using one this whole time."

"Habit," he answers in a clipped tone.

Does he want to continue using them?

"Ty? If you want to still use them we can, but I wanted to put it out on the table that I'm fine if we don't. It's not always convenient, and I trust you."

He kneels on the bed and then grabs both of my feet, pulling me to him.

Rubbing the tip of his cock along my folds, he

confesses. "I've never had sex without one." One hand runs up my thigh and stops to circle his thumb over my clit. "I want this with you. You have no idea how badly," he groans.

"Fuck me, Ty. I want to feel you inside me bare. Hitting me in all the right spots like only you know how to do. Fuck me hard."

In one swift movement, he impales me with every glorious inch of him. "Fuck, Sadie, can't you see how perfect you are for me?"

"Yes, I feel it." I groan as I meet him thrust for thrust. Agonizingly slow, he draws out each inch until only his tip remains, only to then plunge all the way in and pound me with everything he has. Our skin slapping, sweaty and slippery. Hands roaming, caressing, and groping.

"Come with me sweet girl, I need you to come with me," he bites out each word with a pounding thrust, hitting me right where I need him.

"Right there," I slip my hand where we're joined and rub my clit bringing me closer.

"Oh, fuck that's so hot," he pants.

With my other hand, I snake it between us and squeeze his balls; Tyson shouts out and goes completely still as he unloads inside of me, while I follow along with him. Clutching myself to him as wave after wave of pleasure rolls through me.

Each time with Ty is an experience in and of itself. It seems impossible for it to be better than the last, but somehow, he accomplishes the impossible.

When I'm finally coherent enough to assess my surroundings, Tyson is resting his entire body weight on top of me while placing kisses up and down my neck.

"That was amazing," I mutter, wrapping my arms around him and hugging him to me.

Tyson shifts off me to then pull me to his side. Wrapping me in a Tyson cocoon of arms and legs. Making me feel safe and cherished.

"Best sex of my life and I know it's only going to get better," Tyson agrees.

"If it doesn't, I'm happy with the sex we have now."

He chuckles and starts to rub my back in soothing circles. "Get some sleep because you're going to need it."

"I feel boneless after that. I'm not sure I'll be able to walk even after a full night of sleep. Let alone go to work."

"We can always stay home and spend the day in bed," he murmurs tiredly.

"We can do that this weekend. You can't miss the

day after you get a promotion." I snuggle deeper into his arms.

"You're so sensible," he grumbles, kissing the top of my head.

As I'm falling asleep, I swear I hear him say something that sounds a lot like the best night of my life.

16

TYSON

SADIE HUFFS AND BLOWS A LOCK OF HAIR OFF HER FACE. When she hears my chuckle, she glares over the box she's carrying at me.

"You didn't have to help. I could have packed up and moved everything," I say around the three boxes stacked in my arms.

Even though I've been so tired over the past week, I've done nothing but eat, sleep, and work.

Last night I fell asleep almost immediately after dinner. I saw the worry on Sadie's face when she woke me and urged me to go up to bed.

"I know I didn't have to help, but I wanted to. The faster this is done, the faster we can do other things," she smiles slyly over at me.

It has been more than twenty-four hours since I've made her fall apart underneath me, and my Sadie is jonesing for her next fix.

"We can leave the rest in our cars and come back for it later if you want," I suggest as we make our way around my SUV.

"That's very tempting," she stops walking to peek at me from behind her box. "I'm not sure I'm going to be willing to let you out of bed for the rest of the day so…" she nods to herself. "We should probably finish taking your stuff inside. It's not that much."

No, it wasn't. I had very little and donated most of my furniture, so I only had my clothes, books, and computer equipment. All of my toiletries had migrated over to Sadie's in the past month with at least half of my clothing.

"Who's the boy toy?" A whiny female voice asks from somewhere in front of us.

Sadie jumps and pales in the same moment. Her hands grip the box she's holding in a death grip. "Fuck," she swears under her breath.

"Sadie?" I ask, worried by her reaction.

"It's my mother," she grumbles and then stalks off toward the front of her house.

This should be interesting. From what Sadie had

told me, she rarely spoke to her mother, and her mother didn't know where she lived. Until now.

Setting the box down on the sidewalk, Sadie puts a hand on her hip prepared for battle. "How'd you find out where I live?"

The woman sitting on the top step of the front porch sneers at her daughter. Her hair is scraggly and completely gray, her face all wrinkled and leathery. She looks nothing like the woman I've come to love.

Love?!

If I was honest, I knew that I had loved Sadie for some time now, but I hadn't admitted it to myself. Afraid that if I did, then I wouldn't be able to keep it to myself and Sadie would run for the hills.

"Your husband told me," she answers and then cackles to herself.

"Ex-husband and you know it. Don't start shit, Mom," Sadie says exasperatedly.

"I don't know what you did to turn that man gay," she shakes her head. "Are you sleeping with this one? Are you going to turn him gay too?"

I step forward and block Sadie from this evil woman's stare. "All right, that's enough. You need to leave. You're not welcome here."

"Shut up boy, I'll leave when I'm good and ready. I haven't gotten what I came for." I watch as she stands unsteadily and hope she doesn't fall down the stairs and we have to deal with her longer than necessary. The corner of her lips quirks up as she asks, "Who are you to tell me what to do?"

Sadie's shaking hands ball up the back of my shirt as she presses against me. I can't believe her ex gave up her address to this woman. What an asshole.

"I live here that's who," I growl at her.

"Really, Sadie, he's young enough to be your child."

Moving around to stand in front of me, I can feel the anger rolling off Sadie as she stands off against her mother.

"Enough, Mother. It's time to leave. I'm not giving you any money now or anytime in the future, no matter how much you harass me. If I see you around here again, I'll call the cops and get a restraining order."

"Against your own mother?" The woman shrieks.

Hanging her head, Sadie sighs loudly enough for the neighbors to hear. "You're not a good mother. Never have been and never will be, so don't try to guilt trip me. I've given you more than you've ever given me."

"I gave birth to you! You ungrateful bitch," she shouts. Her wrinkly face contorting into rage.

"It's time to forget my address and phone number and calling me at all hours of the day and night to get money from me because I'm done," Sadie states calmly.

"You don't answer!" Her mother cries out.

"Because you only call when you want something and that something is *always* money."

Her mother's face starts to turn red and when it gets to a dark shade of purple, I start to worry that she's having a heart attack or something, but Sadie only shakes her head sadly.

"Stop. If you pass out, I'm not calling you an ambulance." Turning to me, Sadie grimaces and picks up her box. "Ignore her. Let's get the rest of your stuff inside and try to salvage what's left of this day."

"Hey," I stop her with a hand to her arm as she starts to pass me. "Are you okay?"

"Yeah, I will be. Are you okay?" she asks, walking slowly into her garage and stepping into the kitchen.

I have a feeling she's not talking about the show I just witnessed on her doorstep, but the steadily increasing exhaustion I've been experiencing over the past couple of weeks. I've seen the worried glances she's given me.

"I'm good. If you want, you can stay inside, and I'll get the rest."

She silently appraises me, trying to decide what she

should do. I know she wants to help me, but at the same time doesn't want to see or hear her mother.

"I can't let you deal with her on your own, that wouldn't be fair. She'd probably accost you out on the sidewalk, and I'd never see or hear from you again," she jokes as she places the box she'd been carrying down.

Throwing my head back and laughing, I look down at her through my lowered lashes. "There's no way in hell that woman could ever kidnap me."

"She's surprisingly wily when she wants to be. She probably has chloroform in her purse ready to take out any unwilling participants so she can steal their money to get drunk and gamble."

Setting the boxes down on top of the counter, I gather Sadie in my arms. "I won't let anything happen to you or me. I promise. I'm fully capable of getting the rest of my things."

Leaning down, I swipe my tongue across her full pouty lips willing her to open for me. Sadie doesn't deny me, meeting my tongue with hers, and wrapping her arms around my neck to pull me closer.

We kiss for a long moment until we hear a commotion on the front porch and pull apart.

"God, I love kissing you," she sighs against my lips.

A stupid grin takes over my face and kiss her one

last time. "I love kissing you too." Taking her hand to lead her to the garage door, I pause, stealing myself before I open the door, ready for whatever her mother says and prepared to stand up for the most amazing woman in my life.

As we pass by Sadie's silver BMW, we hear a shuffling on the other side of the car, and then a loud scraping sound.

I think she's keying Sadie's car!

"You have got to be kidding me," Sadie mumbles under her breath. "Do you really think keying my car is going to convince me to give you money?"

Popping up on the other side, her mother purses her lips before an evil sneer takes over her face. "Stop being such a little bitch, Sadie, and give me the money. Look at this shiny new car and house. It's obvious you can afford it."

Sadie's face turns red as she turns to look at her mother across the other side of the car. "I've worked my ass off for everything that I have. I put myself through college and worked sixty hours weeks for years. All my hard work gave me this house and car, with no help from you!" Sadie yells and puffs out her cheeks before turning toward me. Her chest rises and falls rapidly, her gaze scanning the houses that line the street.

Hanging her head, she speaks softly not meeting my gaze. "Let's get the rest of your things."

"You can't dismiss me like that," her mother squawks, peering over the roof of the car. "This isn't the end."

"It's over. You can either leave on your own accord and never come back, or I'm calling the cops. This is your last warning."

Wrapping my arm around her shoulders, I pull Sadie to me and kiss the top of her head. "Go back inside. I'll get the rest while you take a nice relaxing bath."

A lone tear escapes when she tips her head back to look up at me. "I want to help."

"I know you do, sweet girl, and the way for you to help me is for you to go inside where I know you can't hear what she's saying."

"If she…" she starts, but I interrupt her. Her sad eyes blinking up at me.

"If she doesn't leave, I'll call the cops myself. I promise." I hug her closer to my side and she wraps her arm around my waist.

Getting up on her tippy-toes, Sadie places a soft kiss to my jaw and then my lips. Whispering, "Thank you."

"Anytime," I answer, turning her back toward the house.

I stand facing off Sadie's mother from across the car until Sadie's inside the house and I know she won't be able to hear what I say.

"I'm not going to let you break her. I don't know how you convinced her ex-husband to give you her address, but you need to lose it. If you don't, you'll regret it."

"Who do you think you are to threaten me?" she growls out, her voice rough.

"I'm not threatening you. It's a promise. Never again are you going to hurt your daughter." I grit my teeth thinking about the sadness I saw in Sadie's eyes only moments ago.

"You don't know what you're talking about," she grounds out.

"Sadie told me enough about what her life was like with you, but that's over now."

She rolls her eyes, "You'll be gone next week. You might as well leave your shit in your truck because you'll be packing it up again."

Not if I have any say in the matter.

"Too bad for you, I'm never leaving."

"Oh," her gray eyebrows pop up in surprise. "Did you get her pregnant? Way to go. It's more than that husband of hers ever accomplished."

My heart sinks into my stomach at the thought that

I'll never be able to get Sadie pregnant. Never round with my child.

It doesn't matter though. If she wants a child, we can adopt or find a sperm donor. Whatever it takes if she decides that's what she wants.

"Oh, by the look on your face, I guess you're just as incompetent," she cackles, her old face wrinkling even more with her laughter. "Well, keep trying if you want to keep her in your life because it won't take her long to see the light and realize that you're much too good for her."

Even though I was taught to respect my elders, it's nearly impossible to do at the moment. It's taking everything in me to remain in control, but I won't let her win.

Instead I start to walk away, turning to look over my shoulder at her. "By the time I get back with my boxes, you better be off the property."

Her face scrunches up in disgust or protest, I don't know what, but she doesn't say a word. After a few minutes of trying to stare me down, Sadie's mother finally gets the hint that no one will be giving her what she wants at this house, and stalks off across the yard and down the street.

I make quick work of bringing in my boxes and taking everything upstairs to find Sadie has cleared a couple of drawers for me, and space in the closet. It hasn't been lost on me that the house is in immaculate shape twenty-four seven and I don't want to cause any undue stress on Sadie, so I take the time to put my clothes away and put away as much as I can without bothering her in the bathroom.

From time to time, I hear the water splash and a near constant stream of vanilla and lavender have been wafting through the crack in the door. My steps quicken so I can join her.

I stand stroking myself, my eyes raking over her voluptuous body. She must sense me in the room because a slow smile spreads across her serene face.

"Are you going to join me? I can warm up the water."

"That would make it difficult to do what I want to do to you," I answer, my voice low and husky.

"Oh, and what is it you want to do to me?" Her eyes blink open and darken the moment she finds me touching myself. Sadie bites her bottom lip hungrily.

"I want to eat your pussy until my face is coated in your cum," I growl out, squeezing the tip of my already throbbing cock.

"Who am I to deny your wish?" she purrs. Slowly Sadie stands, and I watch transfixed by each water droplet making its way leisurely down her body.

Continuing to stroke myself, I let her come to me. It's as if I have a magnetic pull bringing her into my orbit. Her eyes are locked on my hand as her tongue slips out and glides along her lower lip making me harder for her.

Squeezing my cock, I let out a low groan. I could come from only watching Sadie make her way to me. She has no idea how sexy she is. Firm, creamy white breasts that fit perfectly in my hands as well as my mouth, dusky nipples that stand at attention just for me, a trim waist that leads down to the best tasting pussy I've ever had the pleasure of devouring. All of that on top of the toned legs that seem to never end.

She's perfect for me, and I'm never going to let her go. Not if I can help it.

As Sadie steps to me, wrapping her hand over mine, matching my pace, it takes everything in me not to coat her perfect body in my cum.

Peering up at me through long lashes, her whiskey colored eyes heated, her voice is husky and pure sex. "Before you, I'd never watched a man touch himself. It's so fucking hot, I want to combust. God," she sighs, one hand traveling up to knead her breasts. "What you do to me."

Lifting her off her feet, I carry her into the bedroom and place her down on our bed. My body covering hers as I start to kiss, lick, and nip my way down her taut stomach. "You have no idea what I want to do to you."

"Please," she begs, squirming underneath me. "Do what you want to me."

My tongue rims around her cute little belly button and then I descend, placing open mouth kisses to her mound. Running my hands up her thighs, I grasp her hips, and lift her until her pretty pink pussy is right there waiting for me. Already wet and dripping just thinking about what I'm going to do to her.

Flattening my tongue, I lick from her ass crack all the way to her sensitive nub and swirl my tongue, kissing and sucking. Fingers tangle in my hair, pulling and pushing me where she wants my mouth as I devour her. My tongue slides over her slick lips as I push two fingers inside her heat. Pumping first fast and then slow, I rub against the spot that drives her wild. She doesn't deny me as she starts to thrash her head from side to side, moaning, and grinding herself against my face. I lap up her honey as she clamps her thighs around my head.

"Oh, God, Ty. Oh, God. Don't. Stop. Please. Don't. Stop. I'm so close." Each word a moan, a prayer.

I don't stop. I don't answer her, even if I could break away from the hold she has on me. Instead I speed up my actions, adding another finger and driving them in and out faster and faster and then, when I feel her start to clamp down on my fingers, I take her clit between my teeth and nibble.

Sadie lets out a scream that I swear rattles the windows, her head thrown back, hands and thighs clinched tight around my head. But I don't stop. I leisurely lap up every bit of her sweet honey while she slowly comes down.

When she finally releases me from her hold, I kiss my way up her body taking a detour to worship those perfect breasts of hers.

Slipping my tongue into her waiting mouth, I'm met by hers. It's unhurried and in itself almost an act of love making. It's taking everything within me not to tell her how much I love her.

Now is not the time.

Although I have no idea when the perfect time is to tell the woman who means the world to you that you love her beyond measure.

Pulling back, I place soft kisses all over her face. A serene smile graces her face as she lays there with her eyes closed, her hands caressing my back, and arms.

Eyes slowly opening and shining with what could only be love, Sadie cups my cheek. Her voice slightly hoarse. "Holy fucking shit, Ty. That was... spectacular.

If I died tomorrow, I'd be a happy woman. I want that for my birthday and Christmas, and every day of the week."

Rubbing the tip of my cock against her slick pussy, I press against her opening. "I'll happily do it every day of the week."

"I'll take you every day of the week," she moans as I push inside her slick, tight heat.

"My sweet Sadie, you've got me. Day and night for as long as you want me," I slowly withdraw to the tip, and drive back in little by little, feeling her walls pull me in just as greedy for me as I am her.

Resting on my forearms, I make sure with every thrust, I hit her already sensitive clit. My mouth descends on hers, our tongues dancing to the same beat as our bodies. Her arms wrap around my back, her hands wrapping around my shoulders, holding me close.

Pleasure shoots down my spine and my balls tingle.

"I'm close. I need you to come with me," I say, slamming into her.

The moment her tiny hand snakes between us and starts to circle her clit, I feel her walls spasm.

"Let go. I'm so close," she moans out, clinching me tighter.

I thrust once, twice, a third time, and still as I spurt load after load. Sadie milking my cock for all it's worth.

Pulling me down to her waiting mouth, she kisses me sweetly and then sucks on my bottom lip.

"Best sex ever."

I agree.

17

SADIE

"Ty," I NUDGE HIS SHOULDER FOR WHAT FEELS LIKE the hundredth time that morning. "Come on. You've got to get up. It's almost time to leave for work."

He doesn't respond. Again.

"Tyson," I say louder, but nothing. "Tyson Aaron Jacobs," I say loudly against his ear with a note of hysteria.

"What, Sadie?" he mumbles.

"It's time to get up for work," I demand, shaking his shoulder.

"Just a few more minutes," he says before turning the other way.

"No, not a few more minutes." I move to the other side of the bed, so I can see his face. Even after almost ten hours of sleep he still looks tired. "You've been telling me that for the past hour."

One eye opens to peek at me. "I have?" he asks as if he doesn't remember the ten other times, I've tried to get him out of bed this morning.

Letting out a deep breath, I sit down on the edge of the bed and pull his hand to my lips. "I'm worried about you." I kiss the palm of his hand. "You've been so tired lately."

He yawns around his words. "It's nothing to worry about."

"Too late because I'm already worried," I state and bite my bottom lip. Hesitantly I ask, "Is this you not wanting to be worried because of what it could mean, or are you really not worried?"

"For fucks sake, Sadie, I'm just tired." He jumps out of bed all the while growling his ugly words at me. "It happens to everyone. I wake up at the crack of dawn to work out before heading to the office where I then proceed to work nine to ten hours, only to come home and fuck you until all hours of the night. It's a wonder I've lasted this long."

"Is this really how you want the day after you move in to go?" I can't hide the shaking in my voice or the tears that well up in my eyes.

"I didn't think you'd turn all controlling on me the moment I moved in."

He walks to the dresser and pulls out a pair of boxer briefs and for the first time since I saw him naked in that hotel room, I don't ogle him. His perfect body does nothing to me.

"I only wanted a few more minutes of sleep," he spits before slamming the bathroom door.

What the hell just happened?

Had I made a mistake asking him to move in or thinking that he was possibly 'the one'?

I don't wait for him to get out of the bathroom. Instead I pour myself another cup of coffee into a travel mug and head out the door to make it to work a few minutes before everyone else on the floor arrives.

IT ISN'T UNTIL HOURS LATER, AFTER STARING AT MY computer screen the entire day and seeing nothing, that Amanda knocks on my door.

"I'm sorry to interrupt, but I wanted to let you know that I had to cancel your one o'clock meeting with the Johnson team. Mr. Jacobs called in sick, and Ms. Andrews said she was going on a bathroom break and never returned.

He did?

Was it possible that he called in so he could move out and I wouldn't know?

Where the hell did Amy run off to?

"Thank you for letting me know Amanda. If I don't have anything else for the day, I think I'm going to work from home."

She blinks at me in astonishment because I never work at home, but today I'm going to, or at least that's my excuse to see if Tyson's there.

"You have an important email from upstairs."

"Oh, how important?" I ask with a raised brow.

"I couldn't read it. The document is password protected," she answers back, chewing on her bottom lip.

"Thanks for letting me know. I'll check it out and then be on my way. Anything else?"

"Nothing else that you can't do from home," she answers. "Is there anything you need from me?"

"No, thank you. Why don't you call it a day too? You deserve it."

"Thank you, Mrs. Frost. That would be… nice. Thank you."

I wave my hand dismissing her gratitude. "Get out of here before I change my mind."

She hasn't moved from the door since she stepped

inside and now eyes the door as if she's locked inside and won't be able to leave.

Turning back to my computer, I log in to my email and immediately see the email Amanda was referring to.

To: Sadie Frost <sfrost@mathers.com>
From: Brad Sargent <bsargent@mathers.com>
Subject: Amy Andrews Termination

Dear Mrs. Frost,
I wanted to let you know that after reviewing
the security footage of further incidents of theft,
we have found the culprit. Amy Andrews was
seen stealing laptops on two different occasions,
and was fired earlier this morning. You will
need to find replacements on any jobs she was
working on by the end of the week.

Brad Sargent
Head of HR
Mathers Inc.

FOR THE FIRST TIME THAT DAY, I SMILE. I CAN'T BELIEVE that she was stupid enough to be stealing laptops from the company.

I gather my laptop, files, and purse. My mind is a whirlwind of questions and beginning to form a headache.

Why did Tyson go off on me this morning?

Was seeing and dealing with my mother too much for him?

Did he skip work to move out?

Why had he been so tired lately?

Had his cancer come back?

Unsure of when Amanda left my office, I lock up. When I step outside my door, she's gone from her desk with her computer shut down. It was wise for her to get out before something happened, and I asked her to stay late.

I'm on autopilot as I make my way home. I think about trying to call Ty but decide against it. I don't want him to leave if he finds out I'm coming home early.

God, what if he's done with me?

Even with everything that's been swirling in my head on the drive home, I'm shocked to see Tyson's SUV where we left it yesterday. Parking inside the garage, I know that Tyson will know I'm home. No matter where you are in the house you can always hear it when the garage opens. It's not loud, but it's no sneak attack either.

Once inside, I quietly look around the first floor, but there's no sign of Tyson, or that he's been downstairs. Usually he leaves a coffee cup on the counter or a bowl from his granola in the sink, but there's nothing. Taking off my heels, I silently make my way upstairs. My office is the first room I come to, but as I peer in its empty except for a few boxes of Tyson's things he has yet to unpack.

My jaw drops open when I find Tyson asleep on top of the bed in only his underwear. It's now a little past two o'clock, meaning I've been gone for seven hours. Had he been in bed this whole time? Obviously, he was up when I left and at some point called in to work.

I'm not sure what to do. Do I wake him up and try to talk to him? After this morning I'm less inclined to try, afraid of what might come out of his mouth.

"Sadie?" Ty questions quietly, bringing me out of my musings. "Is it…" he trails off, turning to look out the windows to see its still daylight and early in the afternoon. "What are you doing home?"

Crossing my arms over my chest, I stay standing in the doorway. "I could ask you the same question."

He yawns and rolls onto his back to stare up at the

ceiling. He's quiet for so long that I start to think he's not going to answer me.

"Sadie, I'm sorry about this morning and hurting you. I… you're right that I'm afraid of what this could mean. If its… I might…" He takes a deep breath all the while still not meeting my eye.

"Oh, Ty," I make my way across my plush carpet needing to be by his side, fighting back tears.

It's not until I curl up against his side and wrap my arms around him that Ty turns toward me, burying his face in my hair.

"I'm sorry I yelled at you. Even though it's no excuse, I was so exhausted. When I saw the hurt in your eyes, I hated myself which only further escalated matters," he murmurs into the side of my head.

"Are you feeling better now?" I tighten my hold on him.

His only response is to shrug his big body.

"Did you sleep the whole day?"

"No, after I came out of the bathroom and realized that you'd left, I knew what I needed to do," he answers, his voice sad and quiet.

"What did you need to do?"

"I called my doctor and made an appointment. After that I went back to bed to hope and pray… and mope," he admits.

"No matter what the result, I'll always be here for you."

Pulling out of my arms, Ty looks down at me with furrowed brows. "I can't ask you to do that. If I... if I'm sick. You don't know what you're promising until you're in the thick of things. If you think I've been tired this week, you haven't seen anything yet. For you to see me like that..." he trails off staring down at the bed.

"Hey," I place a hand on his firm chest. "We don't know anything yet. When's your appointment? I want to be there when you go."

"That's okay," he shakes his head. "You'd have to miss work."

"You're more important to me than work, Ty."

"Why are you home early?" he ignores my statement, and I let it slide. For now.

"Amanda informed me that you called in sick, and it wasn't like I was getting any work done after this morning. I literally stared at my computer screen all day," I shrug acting as if it was no big deal. "Plus, I wasn't sure if you called in so you could move out while I was at work."

His face softens even as his brows furrow. "You really thought I'd move out while you were at work?" he questions, not hiding the hurt in his tone.

Shaking my head, I shrug. "After this morning, I

didn't know what to think. I thought that if you were going to call in sick, I'd be the first to know about it and not the last."

Hanging his head, Tyson takes my hand in his, rubbing his thumb over my pulse point. "Fuck, I... I fucked up. You most definitely should have been the first person I told I wasn't coming in. Sadie," he looks at me with hopeless, light green eyes and chokes on his words. "What if I'm sick?"

"Then we'll get through it, one day at a time. Our company has great insurance and you won't go into debt paying for treatments."

"I wish I had your optimism, but all I can think about is how hard it was the first time around."

"Hey," my hands cup both of his cheeks and my thumbs stroke along his cheeks. "We don't know anything yet. Let's stay positive until we know for sure. Deal?"

"Deal," he answers back with zero conviction.

Somehow, I need to get his mind off the fact that he very well could have cancer again. Mine too. Even though I've been worried, I'm not ready to contemplate what it could mean if Ty's cancer has come back.

"How about a change of scenery? Are you hungry? I could order whatever you like, make a fire, and we could snuggle up under a blanket and watch a movie or something."

"That sounds nice," he answers, glumly.

Getting up I head to go downstairs but stop, looking over my shoulder when Ty calls my name. "I really am sorry for this morning and making you think there was a possibility I might move out without talking to you first. I'll try my best to make sure it never happens again. Promise."

Tears prick the backs of my eyes. "Thanks."

I walk out before I tell him I love him. When I tell him for the first time, I don't want him thinking it is out of pity.

18

TYSON

WE SIT IN SILENCE. OUR BODIES TENSE AS WE WAIT FOR the doctor to call with my test results.

He's late.

The call is late.

We were told they'd have my results, and he'd call right after two o'clock. I've watched the time tick by second by second, minute by minute for the past half hour, waiting to find out if my world is going to be turned upside down or not.

"Hey," Sadie places her hand on my bouncing knee and then laces her hand with mine. "It's going to be fine. I promise you. I have a good feeling about this."

"Then why is he taking so long to call?"

"Why do doctors always take so long to do anything?"

"You're right."

"I'm glad you've seen the light," she jokes, cracking a smile before her face falls into a serious mask. "Before the doctor calls with your results, I want to tell you something. I'm not sure if now's the right time or not…" She looks around her office briefly before her gaze comes back to mine. "One thing this scare has taught me is to not waste time. You never know what tomorrow will hold."

Sadie's scaring the shit out of me.

What could she possibly have to say, right now?

Bringing my hand up to her mouth, Sadie kisses my palm. "I can see even more worry in your gorgeous eyes. How is that possible," she murmurs to herself, smoothing her thumbs over my brows. "I'm just going to say this, okay?"

"Please," I blurt out in desperation. Hoping for the best but preparing for the worst.

"Tyson Aaron Jacobs, I love you. My heart is full to bursting with what I feel for you. I wanted…"

My lips crash into hers, cutting her off. Our teeth clash and tongues duel as if fighting to say who loves who more.

But she doesn't know I love her.

Breaking our kiss, I pull back and gaze into her shining whiskey colored eyes.

"My sweet, beautiful Sadie," I start, but stop when her cheeks bloom pink. It still amazes me how such simple words affect her. "I love you. I think I've loved you since the first time I saw you in the hallway here, and I promise you that I'll never stop."

"Really?" she squeaks out, her eyes bright.

I can't help but throw my head back and laugh. Only Sadie could make me laugh at a time like this.

A slow smiles spreads across her face and up to her sparkling eyes as she watches me try to gain control of myself.

Pulling her into my lap, I pepper kisses down her nose and along her sultry lips. I pull back enough to lock eyes with her. "Don't act like you didn't know. I'm pretty sure I've done the worst job on the planet trying to hide my feelings for you." I shrug. "Only so you wouldn't run away before you felt the same."

Hands on each side of my face, she smiles brightly at me with shining eyes. "How did I get so lucky? It still baffles me that you're even remotely interested in me and now... you love me," she says the last on a breathy sigh. "At least I got it right before I turned forty."

My heart is doing flips in my chest. She got it right. With me.

"Damn right you got it right," I growl against her full pink lips. Her tongue sneaks out to lick her lips, but

I suck it into my mouth unable to stop myself. I need her more than I've ever needed anything in my life.

My hands travel up the back of her shirt just as my phone starts ringing, and they instantly stop.

This is it.

Wrapping one arm around her to keep her in place, I need her right here with me, I lean forward to pick up my phone from the table and answer. "Hello?"

"Is this Mr. Jacobs?"

"Yes," I answer, trying to swallow the rock that's lodged in my throat.

"Sorry it took me so long to call you, Mr. Jacobs. I had a patient run long, delaying me. I didn't want you to wait until tomorrow. I know you're anxious to know your results and wanted to put your mind at ease instead of keeping you worried for another day."

Did he say, 'at ease'? That's a good thing, right?

"Thank you, Dr. Walters. What do you got for me?"

"Well, the good news is you don't have cancer."

Relief washes through me. I can feel my body sag against Sadie's and like the beautiful person she is, without question, she wraps her arms around me and holds me tight. Supporting me.

My forehead rests against her shoulder as I speak into my phone. "Are you sure? Why have I been so tired then?"

"There is something that's causing your symptoms. Luckily, we took enough blood to run quite a few tests. Although it's rare in men and especially at your age, you have hypothyroidism. I've already called in a prescription for you at your pharmacy, and I'll need to see you in my office in one week for some more blood work. Feel free to look it up on the internet, and I'll answer any questions you have for me when I see you. I want you to know that it's very manageable, but until we get the proper dosage and the right medication you'll be coming in every week or two for blood work. You might want to check with your health insurance to see if they require a lab to draw your blood when it's not included in your well visit. Other than that, do you have any questions?"

Questions?

My mind is blown with the news that I don't have cancer. I thought for sure that it had come back, and I was dying.

"Not right now," I stammer out. "I'm sure I'll have some when I come in."

"Good, I advise you make a trip to the pharmacy before it closes and take your first dose tonight. I don't think you'll have any side effects, but if you have any problems don't hesitate to call me."

"Thank you, Dr. Walters. I'll do that."

"Have a good rest of your day and the rest of your week. I'll see you soon."

"You too," I reply before he hangs up.

I don't have cancer! I don't have fucking cancer!

I'm not dying!

Patting my face, Sadie frowns down at me worry etched across her face.

How long have I been sitting here unresponsive?

"Ty? Are you okay?" Her worried eyes bore into mine. "What did the doctor say?"

"I'm fine. Better than fine," I let out a dry laugh. "I don't have cancer."

"Oh my God that's such great news," she breathes out.

Wrapping her arms around me in a tight hug, I feel Sadie start to shake. I can't tell if she's laughing or crying, or what she's doing until I feel wetness start to seep into my shirt.

"Hey," I try to pull her back so that I can look at her, but she only buries her head into the crook of my neck and holds me tighter. "I promise I'm okay. I have some thyroid problem that I have to start taking medicine for, but that's it."

I don't say what I'm thinking. I'm not dying. That I've been afraid I'm dying since before I went to the doctor.

"I've been so scared," she sobs into my shoulder. "I don't want to lose you."

It both kills and elates me that she was so worried about me. I start to sway as best as I can on the stiff couch, trying to calm her, but in the process all my fears of what could have happened start to surface. Wetness wells up in my eyes, blurring my vision.

Will the fear of a reoccurrence ever go away?

I don't even notice when Sadie sits up in my lap or when my own tears started to fall. It isn't until her delicate fingers start to wipe away the moisture that's coating my cheeks that I'm brought back to the here and now.

"Baby," she kisses my lips chastely. "You're okay."

The only thing I can do is nod my head. The rock that was in my throat earlier is back and brought a few of its friends to take up residence, making it impossible for me to speak.

"Okay," she says softly, nodding her head. She stands from my lap and when I start to pull her back to me, Sadie maneuverers me until I'm lying on the couch where she promptly joins me by placing her body on top of mine and wrapping her little arms around me.

We lay like that for minutes, hours, days. I don't know how long, but the entire time, Sadie never lets go of me.

The only thing I know is I need to marry this woman.

The tips of my fingers inch up her thighs until they're met with the hem of her sexy as fuck short skirt. I slide up her skirt until the globes of her ass cheeks meet my hands where I squeeze and knead their firm flesh.

Slowly, Sadie sits up and starts rocking against my growing erection. I bunch her skirt around her waist, pulling her panties to the side so that my thumb can start to slowly circle her clit.

She rocks against me faster until I'm afraid I'm going to cum in my pants and grip her waist. "I need to cum deep inside of you, not in my pants like a teenager."

Without saying a word, she rises to her knees and starts to deftly unbuckle my belt. In a matter of seconds, she has my cock in her tiny, soft hands, stroking me once, twice before gliding it through her slick folds.

I can't stop the moan that grows from deep in the pit of my stomach as she coats my cock with her juices. With my dick at her entrance, Sadie takes me painstakingly slow, inch by inch. I let her set the pace. After today and everything we've been through, I want to savor the moment and going by her movements, she feels the same way. Taking pleasure in the fact that Sadie loves me. Worshipping the woman in my arms.

When I feel her walls start to pulse around me, my body starts to tingle from my scalp all the way down to my clenched toes. Before I can silence her with a kiss, Sadie calls out my name in a loud moan of pleasure. I stiffen, seizing her hips in my grip as I release inside of her. When every ounce of me has been milked from her tight pussy, I pull her down in a searing kiss. Hot, desperate, and most of all, I can feel her love for me.

Sadie pants against my waiting mouth when we break apart for air. I plant kisses on every inch that my lips can reach. My hands smooth over the silky ivory skin of her back, arms, and ass.

Burying her head in my shoulder, Sadie starts shaking with laughter. What the hell?

Only minutes before we'd been in the throes of passion and now, she can't stop laughing. When she hasn't stopped for over a minute, I'm dying to know what's so funny.

"Sadie?" I ask tentatively, pausing one hand at the nape of her neck and the other at her hip. When her laughter turns into fits of giggles, I'm lost.

"I'm sorry," she sputters out, struggling to sit up from laughing so intensely. "I'm sorry. It's just one of those times…" she laughs into her arm. "When you can't stop." A bark of laughter escapes her clenched lips. "And the more you try the more you laugh."

That's easy to see, but I don't know *why* she's laughing like a mad lady. With each brush of her backside against my semi-erect cock, I'm starting to get hard again. I'll happily take her again in her… oh shit. We're in her office. We've been in her office for who knows how long. Hours? And just made love like we were in the privacy of our own home.

Not her office.

Her laughs die down and she nods. "I think you figured it out. We've been outed by ourselves."

Not the way we wanted it to happen.

At least, Sadie had informed her superiors of our relationship a couple of weeks ago after Amy threatened her, but I know what she's worried about. The looks from everyone, and everyone wondering if I got my job by fucking my boss.

"It could have been better timed," I admit.

She plants her forehead to my shoulder and shakes her head. "I never wanted anyone to hear us having sex. They'll probably install cameras in here after they heard us."

"Baby, they already know about us and yes, this wasn't the best use of our work time, but I don't think they'll install camera's in here. We'll just have to lay low for a while before I ravage you again in your office. We can find somewhere else."

I feel her turn to look up at me and when I look down at her, Sadie's pouting. Fucking adorable. What isn't on this woman?

"Now I'm going to have to be an even bigger bitch to you. Ugh," she rolls her eyes. "I don't even want to think about what everyone will be saying."

"Don't worry about what they'll say. Are you ashamed of your relationship with me?" I'd been wanting to shout it from the rooftops that I was with the hottest woman in the world but had kept my mouth shut in respect for Sadie, and that she would know when the right time would be.

"If you would have asked me in the beginning then the answer would have been yes; I was insecure and felt like a cougar but now," she holds her head up with her hands smiling at me. "I'm proud to call you my boyfriend and to have you on my arm." She frowns, examining my face somberly. "Boyfriend doesn't seem like the proper word to call you, but I don't know what else there is. Lover seems seedy in our case. Nothing I can call you seems to properly convey what I feel for you. What you are to me."

"And what am I to you?"

Without thought, she answers. "My world."

"What about if you called me… husband?"

I keep my face neutral, but inside my heart is beating a mile a minute. Not once had we ever talked about marriage except her failed one. Sadie has never expressed she wants to get married again. Ever.

Blinking at me in surprise, Sadie opens and closes her mouth, and opens it again for it to hang open. When she finally speaks, it's barely above a whisper. "Are you asking me to marry you?"

I can't back out now.

"If the answer's yes then yes, I'm asking you to marry me. First, you can call me fiancé unless you want to go to the courthouse or elope."

Stop fucking talking! She's going to change her name, and you'll never see her again.

Her eyes spark with surprise.

"Well," she draws out the word as she sits up, straddling me again. My dick twitches with her pussy so close. "I don't think I have any plans this weekend," she shrugs as if she's talking about the weather, not becoming my future wife. "We could go to Vegas, have a little fun, and find a little white chapel."

"What?" I ask stupefied, blinking up at her in question. Was she saying yes?

"I mean it doesn't have to be this weekend if that doesn't work for you."

"Ummm, today works for me. Tomorrow. Any day of the week works for me if I get to keep you forever and call you my wife."

"Are you sure? I can be a handful. Think of how crazy I am right before my period. Do you want to put up with that for the rest of your life? Because if you marry me there isn't going to be a divorce, even if I make you gay."

I can't help but laugh. There's no way in hell she's ever turning me gay.

"I know what I'm getting myself into," I nod, still unsure if she's being serious or not because never in my wildest dreams did I think it would be this easy to get her to agree to marry me.

"Okay, I'll look at plane tickets. We can leave after our Friday afternoon meeting and come back..." she looks over at her desk deep in thought. "Shit. I hadn't thought that far ahead. We'll probably want a honeymoon, right?"

She's really going to marry me.

"Every day with you is a honeymoon." I don't need a honeymoon. All I need is her in my life and to become my wife. Now that the idea is in my head, I never wanted anything more in my life.

"That's why I'm marrying you. You're so damn sweet. And hot. And a sex god in bed. And..."

I cut her off by flipping her onto her back with me hovering over her.

"Save something for your wedding vows," I laugh.

Lifting a hand, she lovingly pushes a strand of hair out of my eyes. Her gaze soft but searching. "You really want to marry me?

"Without a doubt in my mind. Do you really want to marry me?" I don't want her to do it because only an hour before she was worried I was going to die. This is forever, just as she said. I would never let her go.

"I do," she answers softly, cupping my stubbled cheek. "I never thought I'd get married again, but now... I can't bear the thought of not being your wife. Not being with you forever."

Me neither.

19

SADIE

TYSON GRUNTS FROM BESIDE ME, AND I CAN'T HIDE THE smile that spreads across my face.

"It's not fucking funny. I should've suggested we go to a private island for our honeymoon, not stay in Vegas. Every fucking guy in a three-mile radius is looking at you," he growls, slipping his sunglasses over his murderous eyes. "I'm going to end up spending my honeymoon in jail. Maybe we should visit one of the shops and get you a full piece swimsuit." He shakes his head. "No, that won't be good enough. You need a Mumu, that way no one can see your body."

Rolling my head on the lounger toward him, I fight to hide my smile, but I know I fail when I can see his eyes turn to slits underneath his sunglasses. "Tyson

Jacobs, I never would have thought you'd be the jealous type."

"I am when every man here wants to fuck my wife," his scowl deepens. "Stop smiling."

"The only person I want to fuck is you, my sweet husband. You have nothing to worry about. Give me half an hour longer in the sun. I'm not as lucky as you. You spend twenty minutes outside and turn a beautiful bronze. I've got to spend hours to get half the tan you have."

It really isn't fair how easily he tans. It only makes him more gorgeous.

Reaching over, he links his hand with mine. "You're beautiful just as you are. There's no need for a tan."

"Thank you, baby. Just give me a little more time and then we can stay in our room for the rest of today. I promise."

If I thought we had a lot of sex before, it is nothing compared to now. Ty's ring now sits on my left ring finger, and it seems to be an aphrodisiac. Every time he gets a glimpse of it, he strips me and fucks me wherever we are. Well almost everywhere. If we're out, he waits until we get into our room where he ravages my body until I'm sated and blissed out, unable to move.

"I'm going to fuck you so hard and mark you every way I can," he growls, pulling my lounger closer to his.

"I'm looking forward to it."

Glancing out to the pool and the surrounding people, no one is looking at me. If anything, it's the women who are all but panting as they take in my husband sprawled out on the lounger like a sex god. If anyone should be jealous, it's me, but I know that Ty would never cheat on me. He loves me and is crazy about me. Which is obvious from his unfounded accusations, but I find it sweet and endearing. It's nice to have someone care about me and want me for themselves.

A few minutes later, I'm all hot and bothered thinking about what Ty's going to do to me when we get to our room, and what he's done since we've landed in Vegas. "Hey, I'm going to take a dip in the pool to cool off, and then we can go."

"I'll come with you," he stands, holding his hand out for me.

I take it, smiling. It's strange to be out in the open with our relationship. The few days we were at work past week after everyone found out about us, we came and left work together and had lunch, but besides those times we kept our distance, trying not to tempt fate and have someone say something that would set either of us off.

On a couple of occasions, I found Ty in a deep 'discussion' with a co-worker, but I let him handle it. It was what we had to deal with now that everyone knew about our relationship. I heard the snickers and the nasty comments behind my back but chose to ignore them as best as I could. I couldn't wait to see the look on their faces when they realized we were married.

Slipping into the water, I glide out to the middle of the pool, cooling off my overheated skin. Dipping underneath the surface to slick my hair back, I emerge to find Tyson standing in front of me, dripping wet. His body glistening in the sun as water droplets trail down his washboard abs. Pure sex.

Biting my bottom lip, I want to run my tongue all over his body. Take him in my mouth and bring him to his knees.

"Sweet girl, you've got to stop looking at me like that or I can't be accountable for what I do to you in public," he growls sexily.

"Come down here with me," I purr.

Sinking into the water, Ty erases the space between us just as I wanted him to. Wrapping my legs around him, I lean back letting my upper body float and look up at my husband. The sun behind him makes it so I can't see his handsome face, but I've stared at him and memorized his features enough that it's as if the sun isn't blinding me from his beauty.

His hand spans my stomach, moving up between my breasts, and back down. "I may not like all the men wanting what's mine, but you do look damn fine in this bikini." His fingertips brush the underside of my left breast before moving around to my side to play with the strings of my bottoms. "I can't wait to untie these strings and let it fall to the floor."

I sit up, keeping my legs wrapped around his waist, and run my hands up each ridge of his spectacular six pack. I don't stop until my breasts are firmly pressed to his chest and my arms are wrapped around his neck, my fingers playing with the hair at the nape of his neck.

Kissing along his jaw, my tongue smooths over his bottom lip. Our tongues dance slowly and lazily. Hands roaming across warm soft skin, over tight muscles. We're out in public, and if we aren't careful, the situation could get out of hand. But in that moment, I don't care. I'd let him fuck me right here and now, except I don't want anyone else to see what's mine.

"What else are you going to do to me?" I hum against his lips, tempting fate.

"Worship every inch of your tight little body. Fuck you with my fingers and mouth until you beg for my cock," he growls before nipping my bottom lip, and then sucking the pain away.

I want to beg him now to feel his cock inside of me.

Even though I'm the one who asked to stay a little while longer at the pool.

Placing kisses down the column of my neck, his hands grip my ass, squeezing with each nip and suck. "I need you, Ty."

"Are you ready to go upstairs?" he asks, biting softly on my earlobe.

"Yes," I answer breathily, trying to fight the need to grind against him. My core pulses with the need to feel him inside of me. "You've turned me into a nympho," I add as I slip down his body.

"My nympho," he laughs, wrapping my hand in his large one, and all but drags me out of the pool.

He doesn't stop as we pass our loungers with our stuff beside them until I stop, jerking him to a halt.

"What?" he asks, looking down at me in confusion.

"We can't leave our phones down here. Someone will steal them."

Ty looks around and scowls. "Put your cover up on."

I giggle like a love sick teenager, but do as he asks, or more like demands, while Ty stuffs my beach bag with our towels, his shirt, and our phones.

When I hear a few giggles, I turn to see a group of college age girls ogling what's mine. I don't blame them. Tyson is model perfect with his long, lean body.

His muscles bulging in the most appealing ways as he rushes to grab everything. He's tanned to perfection making his light green eyes stand out even more. Even a few men chuckle when Ty grabs my hand again and starts dragging me toward the hotel's doors.

"Ty," I admonish him.

Still striding forward, his grip tightens. "Sadie, if I don't get you in the privacy of our room, I'm going to take you right here for everyone to see."

"Hell yeah," some guy off to the side yells as we pass by.

"Take me to our room," I demand breathily, walking faster.

THE MOMENT THE DOOR SWINGS OPEN TO OUR ROOM, Ty pushes me up against it, his hands sliding up my thighs until they meet the ties of my bikini bottoms. With a pull on each side, they pool at my feet. Ripping my coverup over my head, Ty's fingers slip around my neck to undo my top before falling to his knees.

His nose grazes my bundle of nerves and my head falls back against the door from that one touch alone.

"You smell so fucking good."

The tips of his fingers skate up from my ankles until

they grip my hips holding me in place. Throwing my left leg over his shoulder, I tangle my fingers into his hair as his talented tongue swipes through my folds, ending with a swirl to my throbbing clit.

"Grind your pussy into my face. Take what you want," he growls, slipping two fingers into my core.

With his tongue licking and swirling and his fingers pumping, I nearly buckle from the pleasure. My toes curl, heat travels down my spine straight to my pulsing walls as light explodes behind my eyelids.

When I can open my eyes and move my limbs, I slip my leg from Ty's shoulder and run my fingers through his hair. Taking my hand in his, Ty stands in all his naked glory.

When did he take off his swim trunks?

My eyes rake down his torso that's rising and falling as rapidly as my own. I take his length in my hand, stroking its velvety softness over hard steel.

I want him in my mouth. To taste his salty goodness.

Kissing down his chest, I nip down one side of his 'V' and lick down the other.

Looking up, I find Ty's eyes hooded with lust as he gazes down at me while biting his lower lip. His eyes slam shut as I swirl my tongue around his tip and then lick down the thick vain on the underside of his cock.

Taking his length in my mouth, I slowly bob my head and hollow my cheeks.

"Fuck, your mouth is almost as good as your pussy," he grates out, pulling my hair back to get a better view.

I keep taking him until he hits the back of my throat and do my best to swallow him until my lips touch the base of his thick cock. Pulling back, I run my tongue along the underside driving him mad.

Replacing my mouth with my hand, I pump as I lick along his length to his balls. Taking one in my mouth, I lightly suck and lick.

One minute I'm on my knees and the next I'm hoisted up into the air over Tyson's shoulder.

"What happened?" I ask out of breath. My eyes train on the delectable ass in front of me and I can't fight the urge to bite on his firm ass.

"Fuck woman, your mouth is driving me wild. I don't want you on your knees. I want to be buried deep inside of you. You can use your mouth later," he growls.

Bending me over the back of the couch, Ty impales me in one thrust. He leans down until his front is flush against my back, one arm snakes around for his hand to cup my breasts and pinch my nipples. His mouth at my neck breathes heavily. It's not often that we don't have sex facing each other some way, but when we do, Ty lets me know he's right there with me.

Eyes on me.

He's not Gerald.

Far from it, and I know he wants me. Ty makes sure to let me know how much he wants me each and every day.

"I love you," he moans into my ear.

"I love you," I answer back, panting as another orgasm builds.

My fingers dig into the leather of the couch as Ty thrusts deep and hard hitting that special spot inside each and every time.

"Ty," I moan, turning to look at him. "I'm so close. Fuck me harder."

His mouth crashes down on mine. Our teeth gnash, tongues dueling, tasting one another as if it's the first time. I push back as his hips piston into me. His hand slips from my breast to pinch my clit, and I explode. My entire body tenses as wave after wave of lightening shoots through my body until I go slack against the cool leather of the sofa.

Ty thrusts once more before stilling as he shoots his essence deep into my core. His hands on my hips fall to my sides as he slumps down on top of me with his face buried in my shoulder. I can feel his lips tip up against my overheated skin before he kisses me and stands, pulling me up with him.

"I needed that," we say at the same time and then laugh.

Pulling me flush against his chest, Ty gazes down at me with more love in his eyes than I ever thought possible. "Now let me take you to bed and make love to you like you deserve."

Swoon.

Would I ever get used to how loving and sweet he is?

I certainly hope not.

"Sadie," he quietly calls my name making me crack my eyes open to peek up at him. A soft smile tips his lips. "Thank you for becoming my wife." His face is serious and even more severe from the lights of the strip dancing across his skin. "I promise to worship you until the day I die."

"Are you reciting your vows?"

"Don't be a smart ass." He swats my ass making me giggle drowsily.

"Best day of my life becoming your wife," I mumble from my sex induced haze. I'm barely able to keep my eyes open after coming upstairs and having Tyson pleasure me for the past few hours. It is definitely nice to have a husband with his stamina.

Ty's arms tighten around me, and I snuggle further into him.

"When we started this, I thought I was a phase for you," I mumble into the night before kissing his chest. "That you'd get tired of me, and if I opened my heart to you, you'd break it."

"Never," he vows, pulling me impossibly closer to him.

"I know that *now*. You're my forever, and I can't wait to spend the rest of my life with you."

"You've got to stop talking, or I'm going to have to fuck you again." His words and the gravel in his voice make me want to jump him, even if he hadn't already exhausted me earlier. My bones feel like jelly. I'm not sure I could get out of bed even if the hotel was on fire.

Humming, I rub against the leg I'm wrapped around. "I'm spent. All except for my vagina. It has a mind of its own and wants you to fuck me into oblivion."

"That pussy of yours is what brought you to me, so I'll do whatever I can to make her happy and show her how thankful I am that she can't get enough of me."

"She may have started it, but you're now a part of every piece of me. My heart. My soul. My mind."

"Stop talking, Sadie. Let me get a couple of hours of sleep, then I promise I'll be your sex slave if you want," he grumbles, but I hear the humor and love in his tone.

"I could sleep," I say on a yawn. "And I like the idea of you being my sex slave."

His hands cover my mouth and he hushes me with furrowed brows. "I'm serious."

"Me too," I say against his palm. "Now stop talking so I can get some sleep."

Removing his hand, I feel his silent laughter as he engulfs me back into his arms.

"Good night, husband." I smile as I hear his heartbeat pick up pace for a moment, loving how much he enjoys me calling him my husband. "I love you."

"I love you too, my sweet wife."

With eyes closed, I start to doze in the warm embrace of the man I love when I feel him kiss the top of my head and murmur, 'forever'.

After finding Gerald in bed with another man, I never thought I'd find love. Never in my wildest dreams did I think the clumsy intern from work would turn into the love of my life.

The man I can't imagine being without.

My husband.

My forever.

EPILOGUE

Tyson
The Next Spring

I PLACE THE LAST OF THE PATIO FURNITURE AROUND THE pool and look around. The backyard had been a disaster for months as we put in a pool. Technically we didn't put the pool in. We hired a crew, even though Sadie tried to convince me that we could do the job. Maybe if she wanted the pool in about twelve years. I was flattered with her confidence in me, but she has a tendency to think projects are a lot easier than they actually are.

Since I moved in, we'd renovated the rest of the

inside of the house, and once it got warm, she started with the landscaping outside. The first time I came to her house, I only noticed how nice it was, but Sadie started to point out all the things she wanted to fix. She'd hired people to do her bedroom and bathroom along with her living room, since she used those rooms the most and didn't want to wait, but had planned to do the rest herself. We started slowly, but if we weren't at work, or fucking, we were working on the house.

I don't mind though. I love seeing the pride on her face as each room is finished.

The pool was the end game. Now our only plans are to lay out by the pool, soak up the sun, relax outside after work, and watch the hummingbirds as they buzz around the yard.

My first order of business is to strip her naked, go skinny dipping, and fuck her in the cool water.

"Hey, Ty," Sadie calls from around the side of the house.

"Coming," I call back as I make my way to her. She said she had to go get a few more things for the backyard for us to enjoy and had been gone for a few hours. While she was away, I finished setting everything up.

I stop dead in my tracks when the cutest gray puppy, its ears flopping in the wind, comes running toward me, Sadie fresh on its heels.

"Puppy, come back here," she calls, eyes trained on the dog.

Squatting down, the large puppy runs straight into my arms and starts licking my face with abandon.

"Puppy," she admonishes with a scowl on her face.

"Someone lose a dog?" I pick it up and cuddle it to my chest. Its gray fur is the softest thing I've ever felt, and damn its sad puppy eyes staring up at me. I'm instantly in love.

"Not exactly," Sadie mumbles while biting her lower lip.

"What's wrong?" I erase the few feet between us and pull her into my chest as best I can with the dog between us.

She smiles down at the dog with tears in her eyes, and the sight breaks my heart.

"I thought this was a good idea, but now I'm rethinking it. I should have talked to you first," she answers cryptically.

Cupping her cheek, I smile down at her. "You know you can always talk to me."

Nervously she smiles up at me with unsure eyes. "Even after a year it still amazes me how you're the levelheaded one."

"Sweet Sadie, talk to me. What's on that gorgeous mind of yours?"

Her gaze flits around the backyard. Her lips tipping up the more she sees.

"You finished setting up. It looks great," her voice rising in excitement. "I know I've been working you hard to get everything done before the weather gets too warm."

I place my finger to her soft lips to silence her. "Stop. This is our house, and I love the vision you have for it. What's a little work when we can enjoy it for the rest of our lives?"

"Ty," she mouths around my finger, placing a kiss at the tip before she sucks it into her hot, wet mouth.

My dick is instantly hard.

Swirling her tongue around as if it were my cock, she lets it go with a pop.

"Thank you for being you," she softly speaks with tears in her eyes. "Every day I'm thankful that it was you who showed up at my hotel room door."

"What's going on, Sadie?"

She's starting to worry me.

"I see the way you look at the babies we pass by on our walks. The longing, and heartache." She brushes her thumb along my bottom lip. The puppy in my arms and wedged between us, nips at her hand. "And I know we can't have kids of our own, but I thought… well I got us… *you*, this dog."

"Baby, it's not like that. The heartache and longing you see is to see you round with my child. I wish I had known back when I was sick that one day, I'd meet you."

Sadie slips the puppy from my arms and to the ground, wrapping me in her arms. I rest my forehead to hers. The love that I see in her eyes calms the rioting emotions ricocheting through me. Shame, guilt, acceptance, and love.

She plants both hands on my cheeks. "How were you to know?"

"I know, but I wish I had saved my sperm. Even though I didn't have the money to store it. I wish I could give you a child of our own."

"Ty," she coos. "I only need you. I've said it before, and I want you to know that I meant it then, and I mean it now. Only you. You're all that I need, and I hope…" she trails off, looking down.

"You're all that *I* need. I promise. And if you ever change your mind, we can adopt, or find a sperm donor. Whatever you want. So," I draw out as the puppy at our feet pulls on my shoestring.

"I got us a dog," she smiles down sweetly at it. "I've been thinking about it now that the weather's getting warmer. I've always wanted a dog, but as you know we could never afford anything when I was growing up.

Then I saw a sign yesterday with his cute little face on it, and I couldn't resist."

"How could you resist? I fell in love with him the moment he jumped into my arms. It's a boy, right?"

"Yeah," she answers back softly.

"What's his name?"

"He doesn't have one yet, and I wanted to wait for you." Sadie squats down to rub his soft head and squeals when he licks her face. "Isn't he the cutest?" she asks with awe in her voice and stars in her eyes. "What do you want to name him?"

"You want me to name him?" I'd never named anything in my life. I don't want the poor dog to have a shitty name all its life. "Why don't we name him together?"

She tilts her head, looking down at the new member of our house. "He needs a strong name because he's going to be huge." Chewing on her bottom lip, Sadie's hands twist together. "Is that going to be okay? I should have asked you if you even wanted a dog and then talked to you about what type you'd want."

"Sadie," I pull her into my arms, flush to my body, and brush my lips across hers. "He's perfect. You've got nothing to worry about."

"Good, because I already love him. He's so sweet,

and he already listens… and knows some commands."

I love seeing her like this. So happy and hopeful.

"What about… shit this is hard. Who knew naming a dog would be so difficult?"

Certainly not me.

"Do you like Greek mythology?" she asks, scratching behind the puppy's ears.

I shrug. "I don't really know much about it."

"Oh," she nibbles her lip. "When I was in high school, we had to read Homer's Odyssey. I loved it. Couldn't get enough of it so I started learning more about Greek mythology. The word Titus means of the giants in Greek."

Titus.

I like it.

"It's perfect for him."

Her lips tip up slowly until she's beaming. And I know that mine mirror hers. Her smile is infectious.

"I think so. It fits him already."

Sitting down, I pull both Sadie and Titus into my lap. "How do you think the backyard turned out?"

"Better than I imagined. It's going to be amazing when all the flowers are blooming, and the water is warm."

"I can't wait to fuck you in the water. To feel it and you surrounding me," I moan.

"Another place to christen," she hums. I can hear the smile in her voice. Leaning her head back on my shoulder, she says, "You know, I can think of another new place that we haven't had sex on."

I follow her gaze over to the area where I set up the loungers.

"How about I take Titus inside and get him settled and meet you over there. I think we can make it work."

"We always figure something out."

Standing, she smiles down at me. "We do."

By the time Sadie comes out of the house, I'm on the lounger waiting for her.

"Oh, I see you started without me," she licks her lips and starts shimmying her shorts down her hips.

"I know how much you enjoy watching me touch myself," I add

"It gets better every time. You, naked in the sunlight, stroking your big cock is … perfection."

Stopping in front of me, her shorts and panties slip down her toned legs and she kicks them aside.

Fuck, she's beautiful.

I squeeze the tip of my cock when she removes her bra and starts to play with her nipples.

"My sweet Sadie, don't tease. Get over here and ride me," I growl.

"I thought you'd never ask."

Straddling me, Sadie places her hands on my shoulders and slowly lowers herself until I'm seated deep inside her.

My heaven.

I trail my hands down to her hips, my mouth on her neck. I suck, lick, and bite until I have her pebbled nipple in my mouth. My tongue swirls and lashes.

"Ty," she whimpers.

I flick my tongue over her bottom lip and then plunge deep inside. She surrenders to me. Completely. Her breasts rub against me as I help her up and down my shaft. Everything about her intoxicates me. Her scent. Her body. The way she looks at me. It all drives me wild.

I can feel her heartbeat speed up. Matching mine.

"Ty."

The sound of my name on her lips sends a jolt of lightening straight down my spine. Her walls start to spasm around me, and she collapses on top of me as I explode inside of her.

"I told you we'd get good use of the backyard," she pants into my neck. She sighs blissfully. "I love you, Ty."

"And I love you."

My forever.

"Happy Birthday, baby."

Did you enjoy Intern? If so, please consider leaving a review on Goodreads, Amazon, or BookBub. Reviews mean the world to authors especially to authors who are starting out. You can help get your favorite books into the hands of new readers.

I'd appreciate your help in spreading the word and it will only take a moment to leave a quick review. It can be as short or as long as you like. You're review could be the deciding factor or whether or not someone else buys my book.

To stay up to date on all my releases subscribe to my newsletter. Each month I give away an Amazon gift card to one lucky subscriber. http://bit.ly/2M3Ci29

ACKNOWLEDGMENTS

My family- your support means so much. Thank you for all of your encouragement and giving me the time to do what makes me happy.

Grahame Claire if it wasn't for you this book would never have made it past the first chapter. Thank you for all your support and encouragement.

Missy thank you for coming up with the perfect name for such an adorable puppy.

To all my **author friends**, you know who you are. Thank you for accepting me and making me feel welcome in this amazing community.

To each and every **reader**, **reviewer**, and **blog** I would be nowhere without you. Thank you for taking a chance on an unknown author.

To **Enticing Journey**, you're awesome! I'm so thankful for how easy you make releasing a book.

ABOUT HARLOW

Harlow Layne is an emerging contemporary romance author.

Harlow wrote fanfiction for years before she decided to write Luke and Alex's story that had been swimming in her head for years.

When Harlow's not writing you'll find her online shopping on Amazon, Facebook, or Instagram or hanging out with her family and two dogs.

ALSO BY HARLOW LAYNE

Fairlane Series

With Love, Alex

Hollywood Redemption

Hollywood Fairytale

Unsteady in Love

Kiss Me - November 15, 2019

Secret Admirer - September 20, 2019

Spiced Holiday Kisses